# FORGOTTEN GODS

# FORGOTTEN GODS

## FORGOTTEN GODS, BOOK 1

ST BRANTON     CM RAYMOND     LE BARBANT

DISRUPTIVE IMAGINATION

*To Michael Anderle, who has inspired a new generation
of independent authors and found it worth
his while to take a shot on us.*

*The FORGOTTEN GODS Team*

SITTING in a shitty dive in Brooklyn Heights, I tried not to stick out like a sore thumb. The place was full of mobster lackeys swarming the dirty bar like locusts in a cornfield. Normally, a leggy, emerald-eyed brunette in knee-high boots wouldn't stand a chance; they'd be on me the second I walked through the door.

Tonight, I was not in the mood to be mistaken for prey. Luckily, the lights were mercifully low.

The bar was so dark I could barely see the guy across the table, but I already knew what he looked like. All these guys were the same. Bulldog jowls, necks like a tree trunk, and a million rings squeezed onto their sausage fingers. Most of that fancy jewelry was of the costume variety, unless the man wearing it was the real deal and high up in the ranks.

This poor bastard was about as low-down as you could get.

He said his name was Frank, although I was sure he thought I didn't remember.

The shot glasses lined up in front of me like drunken soldiers certainly spoke to a night that had gone far beyond the human power of recall. Little did he know I had bribed the man pouring the booze. Half water, half whatever the hell kind of jet fuel we were drinking. So, I was buzzed, but still ready to rumble.

It's not a good idea to be three sheets to the wind when you've got a man to kill.

I put my elbows on the table, cupped my chin in my hands, and smiled at him. He smiled back, all undone tie and slightly crooked teeth. He probably pictured himself like De Niro in his prime—but he looked more like he had just eaten Joe Pesci. The shadow on his jaw made him look even grimier than he already did in the dim light.

I felt a little sick, but I hadn't gotten as deep in this shit as I was by backing down. And I knew I had deeper yet to go. "Tell me something about yourself, Frankie."

The trick was to make my voice as sugary-sweet as possible, the kind of tone that would rot the teeth straight out of your mouth if you let it. These guys ate that shit up, and Frank, bless his heart, was no exception.

His grin spread, and he leaned back in his chair. "I'm an open book, sweetheart. What do you wanna know?"

What I really wanted to know was exactly how much force it would take to shove an open book down his throat. But I had to play nice until he gave me what I needed. After that, all bets were off.

"Well." I looked at my nails, which had been specially

painted for this little charade. "I heard you're pretty famous around here."

He barked out a coarse, phlegmy laugh. He tried to play off the compliment like it didn't faze him, but he couldn't resist puffing out his chest. "I mean, I guess it depends on who you ask."

"Aww, c'mon." I batted my eyelashes. "You're just playing modest."

He downed his next shot and slapped another bill on the table. We were drinking for money, and from the looks of it, he had half his life savings piled up in front of him. A man his size, going against a woman like me—it was an easy bet.

One that he was about to lose spectacularly.

*Joke's on you, asshat,* I thought. *Never underestimate a girl in stilettos and a slinky dress.* "You're way up there with the big boss, aren't you?" I asked, taking my shot and slapping a bill on the table. "No need to be shy about it."

Maybe I was pressing my luck a little, but he was too sloshed to notice.

Frank hiccupped. "Ah, I ain't nothing next to Rocco." He gestured to the money. "This look like a lot to you? If Rocco dropped that kind of cash on the street, he wouldn't even blink an eye." The sleazy grin reappeared. "I'm flattered, though. Really."

"And you should be." I traced the edge of a shot glass seductively, watching his eyes follow the tip of my finger around the rim. "I think you sell yourself short, Frankie. Rocco Durant can't be that big of a deal, can he?"

Again, he wheezed out a laugh. I wondered if he was going to have a heart attack and die right there on the filthy floor. It would have spared me the displeasure of his company, but right then, I needed him alive. I chose my mark with precision. No one else in that hellhole was as likely to tell me what I needed to know.

"Doll face, you best not get caught talking like that. Rocco runs this town." He made a loose fist and banged it clumsily on the table. The glasses jumped, clinking.

"Hey, Frankie!" someone shouted. "You break 'em, you buy 'em, dipshit!" This first-class quip was met by a chorus of guffaws. I caught a strong whiff of mean booze.

A crowd was forming around us, closing in.

I lowered my voice. "I'm sure he's got people like you whispering in his ear left and right," I prodded gently, trying to ignore Frank's compatriots. I didn't like their intent, hungry looks. "What's it like to be the man behind the curtain?"

We were getting warmer. A few more minutes of this kind of talk, and I'd be home free.

Frank's face fell a little bit. The corners of his mouth sagged. He looked down at his giant, meaty hands, and I braced myself for something unpleasant, such as alcohol-induced vomiting. But in the next instant, his expression cleared.

"It's great," he said. "Nobody messes with you if you're with Rocco."

There was a weird flatness in his tone. I brushed it off. Frank's workplace woes weren't my concern.

I shot him a skeptical look. "Don't tell me he looks tougher than you."

The guy smirked. "Now I know you're putting me on, little lady. Maybe thirty years ago, I could've given him a run for his money, but nowadays..." He shook his head. "It takes a special kind of man to pull off that scar. Right across the face." He drew three fingers down from temple to lip, hooked at the knuckles like claws.

I leaned forward coyly to disguise the fact that my interest had just skyrocketed. "Sounds dangerous."

"Too dangerous for the likes of you," Frank replied with a yellowed smile. It was a strange, almost kind thing for him to say. He glanced around the bar, peering through the low light. "You know, he's here tonight. I could point him out if you really wanna see him."

And there it was.

I dropped my hands beneath the edge of the table, upending it in one smooth motion. The shot glasses, not all of which were empty, smashed on the floor around our feet, sending glass shards and cheap liquor everywhere.

As I lunged toward Frank, I reached through the slit in my skirt and pulled the revolver free of its holster. The other flunkies stumbled backward, cheap suits and ties flapping, a flock of squawking vermin.

Someone screamed.

Frank's chair clattered roughly to the floor beneath our combined weight. He stared up at me, bleary-eyed and stunned. I forced open his mouth with the barrel of the gun and shoved it down until I heard him gag. Then I shouted at the top of my lungs to be heard over the chaotic roar that had mounted in the room. "If anyone moves, I'll blow his brains out!"

No one moved, but they didn't stop talking. That was fine by me. I dropped my voice and jerked the revolver out of Frank's craw.

He gasped. "What the hell are you doing? Are you crazy?!"

"Where's Rocco?" I demanded. He blinked, too stunned or drunk to speak. Maybe I'd let our drinking game go on a little too long. I repeated myself more slowly. "Where is Rocco?"

No answer. So, I cocked the hammer with my thumb. The eyes bulged out of Frank's head. I couldn't help but feel a little sorry for the poor guy. I wasn't going to kill him. Every bullet I had was strictly reserved for Rocco Durant.

Of course, I wasn't about to tell Frank that. I let him gape on the floor. He'd stopped trying to fight me off, and I appreciated that. Maybe we could get along after all. Under different circumstances, anyway. At the moment, not a single asshole in that shitty dive was my friend.

The sound of a door opening caused a tense silence to fall in the bar. Frank's popping eyes tracked to the left, and I followed his miserable gaze. A man built like a brick shit-house entered the bar flanked by four of his goons, two on each side. The scar on his sneering mug cut through one icy eye. It wasn't white like scars were in the movies. It was red.

Our eyes locked across the room. His narrowed at me. The crowd between us cleared, as if the entire moment were orchestrated.

And who am I to give fate the middle finger?

I raised my revolver and pulled the trigger.

## 2

I'LL BE the first to admit I'm not the world's best sharp-shooter.

I was never a cop or a soldier, my dad didn't take me out on hunting trips, but I had a natural feel for guns—at least enough to make who I was shooting at take notice. The first bullet embedded itself in the wall just wide of Rocco Durant's goons on the left, puffing out dust from the cheap plaster.

Time in the bar slowed down for a few seconds, but as soon as the shock had worn off, all hell broke loose. I had to scramble off of Frank to keep from being trampled to death by the herd of terrified patrons making for the door. I raised my arm and fired again.

"Shit!" a goon hollered. "Get him out of here! Go! Go!"

The bodyguards closed around Rocco and began to usher him toward a door in the far corner of the bar's back wall. I got up on my knees, clamped both hands on the revolver's grip, and took aim. My last shot zinged off the doorway just before the door slammed shut.

It was my turn to swear. "Shit."

A moment later, I had the breath squeezed out of me by a lunkhead who thought it was a good idea to grab for my waist. "Gimme the gun, princess!"

Fat chance. There were still three bullets left in it, and I wasn't going to waste them on him. My hand shot out along the ground and grabbed the first thing it found—a heavy pint glass that had somehow survived first contact with the floor.

Perfect.

I swung it up in a vicious arc, and it felt like it broke his jaw. He hunched over howling and staggered away from me. I bolted for the door. If I could get out fast enough, I might be able to intercept him.

Focused on catching Durant, I barely even noticed other people had started shooting. A bullet dug a gouge in the floor next to my heel.

My initial reaction was to frown in disgust, but there was no point in surprise. Of course, these people brought their guns. If I had a revolver, they had full-blown assault rifles hidden up their asses. Sure enough, the rattling report of an automatic shook the air.

All the more reason for me to get the hell out of Dodge.

I burst through the exit and into the cold night. My stiletto-heeled boots sounded like firecrackers on the side-walk as I ran around the side of the building. Who cared if he heard me coming? I'd already taken three shots at his ass and missed every single one. Granted, I suspected I'd be in a lot more trouble if I had managed to kill Rocco then and there. But I was prepared to toss caution to the wind. I'd waited to long not to.

After five years of hunting his ass, I should have known better. But my mom always said I was stubborn as a mule.

She'd said it that morning, an hour before she was gunned down behind the counter of the check-cashing business she'd run with my dad for twenty years. The cops found her sprawled on her back, riddled with bullets, the flowers on her dress soaked in blood.

Daddy was half in the open safe. Glasses broken. A single shot in the head. These two wonderful, amazing people who had never hurt a fly, who took spiders outside instead of smashing them like I did, had been killed and left to rot. And the next night, the business they'd built from love and determination went up in a blaze of smoke.

Just because they wouldn't fold to Rocco Durant's boss.

No one ever said so, but I knew Rocco was the gunman, and I had no reason to believe he wasn't the arsonist, too. I had seen him and his cronies lurking around the storefront at least three times a week, and sometimes, my dad would pick up the business phone, listen for a few minutes, and slam it down.

Rocco was like Frank back then, anonymous, just one of many lowlife thugs looking for a way to climb the ranks.

They threatened Daddy, they threatened my mom, and I was sure they threatened me, though the cowards never said it to my face. I had always been tough, even when I was young. So, they left me alone.

It wasn't enough. Now, I was going to make them pay.

I rounded the corner of the alleyway and spotted Rocco's posse running across the dilapidated lot. Usually, he traveled in a blacked-out SUV, but there was no sign of it. I guessed he hadn't been expecting trouble tonight, and I allowed myself to feel the tiniest spark of pride for managing to get the drop on him. Sure, it had all gone south more or less immediately, but I had to take my accomplishments as they came. Leaning forward into my run, I pumped my legs furiously.

One of the goons looked over his shoulder. His eyes widened when he saw me charging across the pavement. His gun barked. I ducked as one bullet, then another, zinged over my shoulder. Two inches from my right foot, the broken asphalt exploded into a cloud of dust. I kept going.

*Nice try, assface. I'm your worst nightmare.*

The flicker of fear I saw in his expression fed something dark and ravenous inside me. If I had never been as compassionate as either of my parents, that warmth died with them. My only goal was to make Rocco Durant feel the same pain that had plagued my life in the years since he murdered the two people who'd loved me the most.

Jail was too good for him. He had to deal with me.

The alleyway opened on a side street that the mobsters clearly expected to be deserted, because they sprinted into the middle of the road, straight into the path of an oncoming car. Their wild, defensive gunfire faded, and the blare of the horn reverberated through my head. Another bullet sang past my ear. Their faces were pasty in the headlights.

The sedan veered to the left, beams flashing across me, and I squeezed my eyes down to slits against the sudden glare. Over the squeal of the tires, I heard a muffled thump.

My heart leapt into my throat. Had Rocco been hit? It wouldn't be the same as cutting him down on my own, but I was still perfectly willing to execute the wounded.

Vengeance was vengeance.

As for the witness in the car? They'd split as soon as they saw the gun. That's how it worked in the movies.

Nearing the narrow intersection, I saw that the victim wasn't Rocco after all. The idiot who had led the pack directly into harm's way was the one to reap karma's just rewards. His cohorts held him up, and he hobbled painfully, perched birdlike on one leg. All four of them caught sight of me and turned to look at their fearless leader.

Rocco brushed dust from a charcoal suit that was much nicer than the ones worn by his underlings. He sneered as the car backed up and roared between us. A cloud of dirty exhaust choked my vision, but I could still hear the boss's voice, smooth and dripping with arrogance.

"Let it go," he told his goons. "You take care of Vincent, you understand me? Bring him to the safehouse, and don't you dare leave him. Now get out of here. I'll handle the broad."

Adrenaline pounded through my veins. Never in my wildest murder-dreams had I envisioned a one-on-one confrontation with the man I'd been preparing myself to face for five long years. I barely remembered who I was before Rocco Durant shit all over my life. And here he was, practically offering himself up like a sacrificial lamb.

The moment the smoke cleared, I was staring into the black eye of his gun. He smirked as he cocked the hammer.

"You made a bad mistake, little girl."

*Fuck that.*

I drew my revolver faster than I'd ever done anything in my life. The shot went wide, but not that wide. Not enough to kill the bastard, but enough to make him miss. Ears ringing, I saw him curse. The familiar wash of approaching headlights illuminated his jacked-up face.

Then he was hauling ass again, suit jacket flapping. Never in my wildest fantasies had I imagined Rocco Durant rabbiting on me like that. I should have known, though. They were all the same: tough on the outside, nothing underneath.

Gritting my teeth, I gave chase again. These heels weren't meant for running. My feet were starting to complain, but there was no way I could give up a chance like this. Besides, Rocco couldn't last forever. He had aged poorly since my parents' death, and he hadn't been young to begin with. Sooner or later, he'd run out of steam.

"It's a dead end, Rocco!" I yelled. Not a good idea. I needed all the breath I had if I wanted to keep running. Part of me wanted to rip my shoes off, but it would give him a few extra, valuable seconds, and going barefoot in this neighborhood was just asking for trouble. The last thing I needed was broken glass to the foot.

So, I kept plugging away, focusing on maintaining my considerable momentum. I hadn't told a lie; it *was* a dead end. The crumbling brick wall loomed up ahead.

If this was some screwed-up game of chicken, Rocco Durant was going to lose, and badly.

He shot off to the right so fast I almost didn't see his shadow disappearing into some secret passage. I skidded to a stop, cursing the air blue. The space where he'd squeezed himself through was barely wide enough for a guy his size to fit; I was almost impressed he could move so quickly.

I threw myself after him. The walls seemed to close in all at once, grimy and full of mildew. I didn't risk looking anywhere other than forward, but I thought I saw pipes crossing over my head.

Where the hell were we? And where were we going?

There was one great benefit of having a single goal, so all-consuming that I couldn't even dream of doing something else. I had a lot of time to think about it. So, I slipped into a familiar headspace as I ran after Rocco Durant down a slot carved between two buildings.

I was twenty-three again, brimming with rage and compressing a flood of angry tears down into a concentrated form of pure hatred. Making Rocco understand what he'd done was a lost cause. It wasn't possible. He couldn't grasp the anguish I felt when I was told the cops couldn't and wouldn't do anything about my parents' murders.

While Rocco and his boys paid every corrupt officer in the borough to turn a blind eye, I funneled my family's savings into lawyers' fees. I had been willing to give anything to bring Rocco to justice. The insurance money. The house. The heirlooms I pawned all over the city.

Anything.

But nothing worked. There was no hard evidence, they said. Nothing beyond a reasonable doubt. My parents' murders were done by a professional who didn't leave a trace.

I was left broke and alone in a city that didn't give a shit about me. So, I decided to take justice into my own hands.

Back then, I didn't know how bloody justice could be, but I learned. I adapted.

Now, I was more than ready to bring the hammer down.

Up ahead, Durant broke free of the crude alley, and I smelled an acrid tinge of saltwater. The docks. My instincts kicked into overdrive. Whatever his crazy plan was, I had to stop him from going through with it and getting away. I wouldn't put it past the scumbag to jump straight in the water, and if he did that, I'd lose everything I'd spent the past half a decade trying to accomplish.

That wasn't going to happen. My fingers found the curve of the revolver grip. I yanked it out of the holster. It was a long shot, but worth it if it landed. I took a moment, breathed, then squeezed the trigger.

The gun bucked, and the report left my ears ringing again. I saw Rocco Durant's stride falter.

*Yes!*

He twisted around and fired back at me. A chunk flew out of the wall a few feet ahead of me. Close, but not close enough. I didn't even flinch as I moved toward him. The hunt was everything, and I would not be dissuaded. If he killed me, I'd come back as a damn ghost and haunt the shit out of him for the rest of his life. That was how determined I was to make this awful prick pay for what he did. Was it more than he deserved?

Absolutely not. He deserved all that and more.

By the time I got down to the river, Durant was hobbling. His left pant leg wet with blood. The lights of the Brooklyn Bridge and the New York skyline lit him up from behind. I leveled the gun and shot again, hitting him square in the shoulder. He let out a harsh bark of pain—music to my ears.

Rocco Durant's suffering had only just begun.

"Son of a bitch," he muttered. "My ankle. My damned ankle!"

He dropped to one knee as I approached, and then he fell, a few feet shy of the end of a pier. Grit and mud stained that expensive charcoal suit. He pushed toward the gray water with his good foot, until I came up and stepped on it, grinding the point of my heel on the bone.

He held up his hands. "All right! Shit, that hurts. For a chick, you sure got some balls, you know that?"

"Yeah, I know." I flicked out the revolver's chamber, spun it, and locked it in again. There was one bullet left, and I had a pretty good idea of where it should go. The space between Rocco Durant's eyes looked like prime real estate to me.

I pointed the steel muzzle at his face.

"Listen." He licked his lips nervously. Sweat beaded on his thick, wide brow. Even prone, he was huge, his chest heaved, and I heard him fumbling for enough breath to form the right words. I'd been right about him; he was getting old. "Listen. We can cut a deal, you and me. How much do you want? I've got everything."

A sick smile formed on his lips. It didn't quite reach his eyes, which were still as hard as the first time I saw him in the bar. "I can make your dreams come true, girlie. Vacation house? Luxury car? Enough money that you'll never have to think about working again? Lay it on me. I'll make it happen."

I clenched my jaw. Listening to him attempt to bargain

for his life only grated on my nerves. As if he could buy his way out after all the ways he had torn my life to shreds.

"You know what I want," I said, cocking the hammer with my thumb. "And I'm about to get it."

Rocco Durant laughed. He laughed so hard his body curled in on itself where he lay. Tears gathered in the corners of his eyes. "Is that what you think talking tough sounds like? I guess I ain't surprised. Your parents were soft targets. Especially your pops." He wiped his hand across his face and grinned at me. "Oh, you think I didn't recognize you? You got a nice, tight shape, just like your mom. How could I not?"

I froze. The hand holding the gun shook with shock and rage. Suddenly, I couldn't seem to muster the strength to pull the trigger. It was like being frozen in the middle of a raging wildfire. Every ounce of my being screamed to kill the worthless piece of human garbage laid out before me, and yet, the mention of my parents had me transfixed.

"Don't you dare say a thing about her." The voice that left me did not sound like my own. It was a feral growl, the snarl of a wild beast. I felt myself teetering on the brink of something vast and searing.

"You know what she said to me that day?" Rocco asked. His tone was maddeningly conversational, like we were old friends reminiscing. "She told me to go to hell." The smile on his mouth turned cruel. "I said I'd be happy to take her with me."

I'd meant to keep my cool, but this was more than I could take. I shoved the barrel of the gun right up against his forehead. "I've been waiting for this for a long time, Rocco."

My trigger finger trembled. He glared up at me, defiant, but then his gaze shifted abruptly. His eyes widened as they focused somewhere over my head. I sensed a deep shadow descending.

I didn't have time for more than a quick glance over my shoulder. A flash of gold and the looming shape of something both large and seemingly on fire blotted out the whole skyline across the river with its brightness. New York's sorry crop of stars had nothing on this monster.

It was heading straight for us.

I had to laugh. Hadn't I seen this in every disaster movie ever made? It looked like the end of the world. But instead of fire and brimstone, the world was washed away by pure golden light.

## 3

WHEN I OPENED MY EYES, it was clear the world hadn't ended. The sky had regained its polluted dull gray, and I could feel the wet of the pier pressing into my skin.

I was alive—and so was Rocco Durant.

The wounded thug was struggling to stand, the blood on his clothing half dry. He looked like death, but that didn't keep him from making a break toward the alley.

"Hey!" I jumped to my feet, ignoring the way the world rocked unsteadily. I leaned in to bolt after him for the third or fourth time that evening, but something in the water caught my eye. I turned, convinced it was a trick of sight, but no—it was real.

There was a guy in the water.

He didn't float for long. As I watched, his body began to slip below the surface. The dark water climbed up over his chin and then his nose.

I glanced at Rocco, still shambling toward freedom, and

back at the sinking stranger. It was impossible to describe how utterly torn I felt in that instant.

On one hand, the revenge I had dreamed about for the past five years was escaping from under my nose. On the other, it was pretty clear that if I didn't do something, this stranger was going to drown. The decision had to be made quickly.

I raised my gun. Maybe I could get off one last, lucky shot.

*No.* The thought hit me so hard it was like it had come from someone else. *Don't waste that bullet. Save it, and save that man.* Running toward the edge of the dock, I pushed off with both feet, and catapulted myself into the depths.

The shock of the cold forced all the air from my lungs. I had to fight not to inhale the water. My open eyes were freezing in their sockets, but closing them was an impossibility. Down below, something shimmered in the blackness. I swam toward it. I wasn't sure how far down I went, but the moment I discerned the shape of his body, I reached out, grabbed him, and pulled with all my might.

One hand wasn't enough, despite his current weight-lessness. I slung his limp arm over my shoulder and towed him to the surface. My legs burned from kicking. The stiletto boots weighed down my feet. I regretted wearing them, but to be fair, taking a dip in the river hadn't made it onto my to-do list.

I came up not too far from the dock, and on my way over to its solid surface, I racked my brain to come up with a plan for lifting this guy out of the water. His lips were already blue. I had to get him warm and dry fast, which seemed like a problem. I was no weakling, but this guy was heavy as shit.

"Dammit to hell, you better be alive," I muttered, spitting water. "I'm not carrying your corpse anywhere."

Once we reached the pier, I treaded water for a moment, considering my options. I could do a Hail Mary heave and hope he'd stay put while I got myself out, or I could scramble onto the concrete first and hope he didn't sink too far to recover. Neither seemed like a good choice.

Holding on to the edge of the dock with one hand, I maneuvered the guy's arm so that it rested flat on the surface, but I couldn't get him to stop sliding back into the water. He was total dead weight, and I didn't have a buoy to hold him up.

My fingers and toes were going numb, I'd swallowed more river water than I cared to think about, and this whole treading-water situation was not going to last forever. So, I chose the hidden third option, which was to pull him the long way down the length of the dock to the actual shoreline. The moment I could stand, I gripped him under the arms and started dragging.

He made a weird metallic rattling in the shallows. I looked down to see that half the reason he weighed so damned much was because he was wearing armor. Not the modern, bulletproof kind, either. This was the kind with plates and chainmail. I frowned. Had I just fished a cosplayer out of the river?

Even hardcore fanboys deserved to be saved.

He was older than I first thought. Shocks of gray ran through his dripping hair, and the lines around his eyes and mouth were deep, or at least, I suspected they would be if he were warm and dry. It was tough to tell anything meaningful about him while his skin was so pale and drawn.

At his side, something glowed—the thing that had allowed me to find him in the first place. I knelt down to get a better look. It appeared to be some kind of handle, about as long as my forearm and heavy. There was real damage potential there, but I could tell it was missing something.

Even out of the water, it glowed from within like live embers. It was definitely the strangest shit I'd seen in a while, and I'd seen a lot of shit.

"You gotta find her now!"

My head snapped up at the sound of voices too nearby for comfort.

"We're gonna take care of this bitch for the boss. And then we're gonna live like kings."

I crouched down beside the still-motionless body of the man I rescued, feeling for the shape of my revolver against my thigh. All I felt was the holster. A white-hot bolt of panic ran through me as I dropped my gaze to find it empty. The gun was probably half buried in the mud at the river bottom by now.

"Shit," I whispered. Once didn't seem like enough. "Shit!"

The second curse pierced the air a little louder than I intended, and a goon turned in my direction.

"Shut up," he called. "I think I heard something."

He rounded the posts at the base of the pier and got an eyeful of me, hunkered down by what appeared to be a corpse, my clothes heavy with moisture.

"Well, well," he said. An oily smirk spread across his ratty features. "Look what the cat dragged in." He put two fingers in his mouth and whistled. The others seemed to materialize out of thin air. "Ain't this a fine how-do-you-do? Fancy meeting you all the way out here."

*Ugh.* I wanted nothing more than for him to stop talking and pick a fight already. All my nerve endings hummed with adrenaline. My heartbeat throbbed in my ears and throat. For the first time, I began to dread that this was truly the end of the line.

That didn't mean I was done fighting, though. Far from it. But I needed a better weapon than my fists.

"What's the matter, sweet cheeks? Cat got your tongue?" The three of them advanced on me.

I glared at the guy who'd spoken, a skinny dude shaped like a pencil. "What is it with you assholes and cats? Are you so obsessed with pussy because you don't get any?" Despite the brave retort, fear crept unbidden into the back of my throat. I heard my voice tremble just a little bit, and I knew they heard it, too.

They were all smiling now, leering. Pencil-Dick put a hand in his pocket. My mind raced to predict what he would pull out. A knife? A gun? Zip-ties and a blindfold? The fact that I couldn't rule out the last option made my stomach absolutely crawl.

"Don't worry, princess." He spoke in a grotesque carica-ture of a soothing tone. "We won't kill you right away. First, we're gonna have some real fun. Do a number on that pretty kitty, you get me?"

Vomit threatened my throat, but I choked it back. No more distance could be put between me and the tight semicircle of mob sharks. The water lapped at my back. Again, I glanced around, searching for something with which to defend myself. The glow of that peculiar handle drew my eyes. I grasped it and tugged it loose from the stranger's belt.

*Sorry, guy. A girl's gotta stay alive somehow.*

The goon triplets took another step closer. Now armed, I raised the glowing object above my head, pleased to note that it did indeed have a substantial amount of heft. It gave them pause for approximately half a second before they burst out laughing.

"What's that?" Pencil-Dick demanded between guffaws. "Your participation trophy for a job half-finished?" He elbowed his buddies.

He was evidently the comedian of the group, because their amusement doubled.

I scowled. "Let's see how far I can shove this participation trophy up your ass."

That got their attention. Pencil-Dick's hand gripped something inside his pocket. He started to withdraw it. The glint of metal peeked between his fingers. I thought I was going to die.

Then, I went blind.

It only lasted a second, but the flash was bright enough to wash out everything white. The handle vibrated against my palm, and I looked up.

A sword.

The thing was a damn sword!

Its blade was shining and golden—the kind of thing you'd expect to see getting pulled from a stone in fairytales

—but it was real. I could feel its dangerous mass just waiting at the end of my reach.

How much force would it take to drive this through something, or someone? Not much, I guessed.

The mob grunts stared, their mouths hanging open and their slack faces bathed in yellow light.

"Do you see this shit?" one of them asked no one in particular.

Pencil-Dick glowered. "Hell yeah, I see it, and I don't like it." He lifted his hand to reveal a stubby silver pistol.

*Now or never.*

I swung the sword downward. Less than halfway through the arc, gravity took over, and the thing stuck in the ground. I might have stared dumbstruck at it forever if it weren't for Pencil-Dick's screaming. Drops of something dark splattered down around the embedded point of the blade. It was blood. Shortly thereafter, I realized he was missing the hand that held the gun.

Brutal, but efficient.

The goon to my left made a move to close in on me. I freed the sword from the dirt and ran it through his stomach. He made a muted choking sound. Red trickled, then ran, from his mouth. On its way out, the gleaming blade sliced cleanly from his gut, up through his shoulder. I watched the body fall in pieces, and I felt nothing beyond a dull satisfaction.

These guys were not Rocco, but they would do for now.

It was Pencil-Dick's turn to crouch, trembling, as his friend attempted to help him stem the bleeding from his brand-new stump. I drew back and let the sword draw a golden curve in the air, straight through his friend's neck.

His head rolled off into the shadows. Pencil-Dick whimpered.

The momentum from that swing carried me through into a spin, and on the return, I cleaved him more or less in half at the waist. I hardly saw him die.

I stumbled a little, caught off guard by the weight of the weapon in my hand. A hush descended on the deserted pier. The moon shone down on me, surrounded by three bodies—four, counting the dude from the river—and holding a sword that was clearly beyond my understanding. My eyes went from the golden blade to the sliced-up goons to the drenched old man, in that order.

"What the *hell* just happened?"

---

THERE WAS no time to wrestle an answer out of my question, because whatever I had stumbled onto, it wasn't done with me yet.

Three dead men lay before me, and a fourth was quickly on his way. I needed to get far away from here, and leaving the old man wasn't an option. Saving him from drowning just to let him die kind of sucked.

So I leaned in, and struggled to drag his waterlogged, armor-clad half corpse toward the relative safety of the street. That safety disappeared as the growling of an engine met my ears.

"Those little pricks just can't resist me, can they?" I muttered. My cargo shifted his weight, nearly throwing me to the ground. "Hey, watch it!"

His head fell to the side, eyelids fluttering. The engine drew nearer. It was circling, no doubt a driver looking for his three partners, who were now resting in pieces around the pier. Sooner or later, he would find us instead. I adjusted my grip in the stranger's armpits and pulled him as fast as I could. "Work with me here. We're running the hell out of time!"

Incoherent mumbling was his only answer.

But I wasn't shit out of luck just yet. There was a junked-out beater at the curb, its edges dark with rust. If it wasn't already abandoned, no one was gonna miss that thing. I redoubled my efforts, the drone of that circling engine humming in my ear. The car—our salvation—inched closer.

Three feet from the driver's side door, I lost patience. Dumping the stranger as gently as I could in a wet heap on the gravel, I bolted to the car and yanked on the handle. The door stuck for a moment before bursting open in a rain of rust and paint chips. Wires already hung exposed from the underside of the steering column like a gift from the Grand Theft Auto angels.

I was hunched over in the front seat when the prowling driver finally discovered us. Just as the beater sputtered to life, someone's feet hit the ground outside.

"Hey, you!"

I jerked my head up, all ready to let the dickhead know he'd chosen the wrong bitch to screw with that night. But he wasn't talking to me.

"Holy shitballs," I whispered. The dude in the armor stood dripping in the spot I'd left him. He loomed head and shoulders over the thugs who were piling out of the car. I hadn't noticed his mean-ass spear before, but I damn sure saw it now.

It looked a lot more menacing in his hands than it should have, crazy getup and all.

He swung the point so fast that it sounded fake, except its trail was laced with blood. My jaw dropped open as the spear danced through the air. It looked so simple—nothing more than a fancy stick with an arrow on the end—but it did some serious work. The man in the armor made death look a little like art; almost beautiful, if no less cruel.

By the time I snapped out of it and realized he was actually committing murder, one of the thugs lay crumpled in a widening pool of his own blood. I tried to keep my eyes from fixating on the place in his throat where the spear gouged. My heart pounded wildly. I'd just gone from perpetrator to witness in the span of ten minutes. And I didn't like that shit at all.

"Hey, Spartacus!" I called. My throat was dry. "We gotta split. Come on!" The dude dragged his spear out of the last goon's chest and started toward me. After two steps, he faltered. After three, he was back on the ground.

Two human beings cut down like blades of grass, and he couldn't last a minute when it counted the most.

Freaking men.

## 4

"SHIT, SHIT, SHIT, SHIT," I muttered over and over again to myself, my curses barely audible over the car's engine.

I was driving down a side street in the shitty Buick that I hotwired on the curb, with the half-drowned stranger shoved in the backseat. It had been an ordeal and a half to get him all packed in there, but grit carried me through in the end. Sure, he was folded like a paper crane, and I had to lean on the door to close it, but I couldn't afford to care. The guy had just knocked off two people like he was out for a walk in the park, and he wouldn't remember any of it anyway. If he did, I'd just apologize.

Assuming he woke up again.

The thought of him lying dead back there filled me with panic, even though he was breathing and had a pulse. If I had the option, I might have taken him to a hospital, or maybe I would have called the cops. But those were privileges for a normal person with a normal life.

Not for me.

Not to mention the fact that I didn't trust a single New York cop as far as I could throw him. They hadn't done shit when my parents died; they wouldn't do shit now. And the hospital staff would definitely call them as soon as they got a load of the armor on this guy.

For better or worse, I was his only hope right now. I didn't want or need that burden of responsibility, but I also couldn't fathom just tossing him in the street, most likely to die alone. I had already saved him from drowning. The least I could do was try to get him back on his feet. Then, maybe he could fill me in on the whole sword thing. That would be nice.

First, we needed to get the hell away from the dock before someone else just happened along. The way my luck was going, it was inevitable. Hence, the stolen car.

This particular set of skills didn't necessarily make me proud, but when you're surviving on nothing but your wits, you have to make some moral compromises. Good and evil had a way of becoming malleable in the moment.

I stopped the car in front of my building. Normally, I would have ditched it much farther away from my place, but he was too heavy, and I was too tired to drag him far. I extracted him from the back, and his legs hit the ground kind of hard. I winced, then figured the armor would curb the worst of the damage.

We still had four flights of stairs to conquer, which was no easy feat. He was a man-sized dead weight, wrapped in chains, and I had to drag him up steep-ass staircases with loose railings.

I dropped him a few times, and on the fourth floor, his head thumped against the landing. I winced at the sound.

"God, I hope you don't remember this." He didn't even move. "I also hope you're not dead. And I wish I spent even *more* time working out, because hot damn."

I propped him up against the wall next to my door and wiped my brow with the back of my hand.

"I know I just killed some guys, but did I deserve to drag three hundred pounds all the way up to my door? I'm not sure."

His head slipped to the side as I hauled him over the threshold. He lay in the middle of the floor while I secured all the locks and walked around my apartment shedding light on things. The wiring in the building was dodgy at best, but I'd long since gotten used to the flickering. Couldn't deny it beat sleeping on the street.

After the workout on the stairs, getting the guy situated on my mattress was a piece of cake. I arranged his limbs deliberately so that he did not look like a body in a coffin, and then, I examined his armor. I knocked on the plate with my knuckles, as if the weight wasn't enough proof that it was real metal.

Where had this dude come from, and why was he dressed like this? I decided I would help him, if for no other reason than to learn the answers to those two questions.

The armor came off in pieces. I laid it carefully on the floor. Underneath it, the stranger was almost shockingly well-built for a guy who looked like he could be a new grandfather.

Yet another mystery.

I was soon distracted by the discovery of an injury, a huge, black wound on the right side of his back. The wound was literally black. It looked like it was filled with ink. Eerie, vein-like lines spiderwebbed out from the center, wrapping around the side of his ribcage.

"I don't think I like that," I said to myself. I went to the tub against the far wall, wet a clean rag, and wrung it out in the basin. When I put it to his skin, some of the black stuff came away. "Well, that's gross—"

He grabbed my hand.

I wasn't one of those girls who screamed at everything, but that did the trick. Out of pure instinct, I seized a vodka bottle from the crate that was my nightstand, and I brought it down on his head. He grabbed his skull with both hands, releasing me, and I jumped back, yelling in a deep, coarse voice.

I brandished the bottle, now broken, in front of me.

"Who are you?" I demanded. My voice had lost a lot of its typical bravado. I'd had a long day, and I wasn't looking forward to whatever this was.

He looked around wildly, searching for something. He almost jumped out of bed, wound and all, until his eyes landed on the golden hilt leaning up against the wall in the corner.

He took a breath, then turned to face me, flinching as his wound wrenched. "You struck me!"

More than angry, he sounded surprised, and maybe even a little hurt. Like I should have known better. *The nerve.*

"Because you grabbed me!" I shook the bottle at him. "Who are you?"

He shook his head, blinking. "I am Marcus. From Carcerum. And you strike very hard."

"Thank you. I don't know what Carcerum is." I kept the bottle out in front of me.

"No, of course you don't. You are..." He trailed off, taking real stock of his surroundings for the first time.

I felt slightly self-conscious about a lot of things: the bare floor that was stained and chipped in places, the exposed light fixtures, the toilet obscured by nothing but a haphazard wall of crates and corrugated cardboard. To say nothing of the punching bag in the corner that was little more than my old mattress wrapped around a pole and secured with duct tape. Or the furniture I'd clearly pulled from other people's junk.

"What is all this?" he asked.

"Look, I know it's not much, all right?" I said defensively. "I'm not in the greatest situation. I couldn't take you to the hospital. I'm sorry."

"Hospital?" He looked at me with genuine bewilderment. "What do you mean by 'the hospital?'"

I stared at him. Either I'd dropped him harder than I thought, or he was really committed to his character. I pinched the bridge of my nose.

"Just tell me what you're doing here. I've had a rough night. And some of it is your fault, so you better have a damn good explanation." It wasn't exactly fair to come down on the guy who'd narrowly escaped drowning an hour before, but I was exhausted and hungry and wanting to put it all behind me so I could move on.

Marcus pursed his lips, thinking. Finally, he said, "I will tell you my story in exchange for yours."

I rubbed my face. "Oh, come on. I'm not the one who dropped into the river out of nowhere and almost died in it. I don't carry around a huge sword made of light or some shit. I don't wear armor!"

He was unruffled. "What is your meaning?"

*Seriously, this guy.* "My meaning is that you have a ton more explaining to do. And it would be cool if you could start that sometime this year." Frustrated, I got up and stalked to the old oak dresser I had painstakingly carted back from someone's curb, not unlike the way I'd muscled Marcus's ass up those steps.

I grabbed a fresh set of clothes. "Don't look. I'm changing."

I had no energy to bother with any more than that, so if he looked, I didn't know. It felt amazing to get into something dry—grey sweats and a well-worn tank. Comfort clothes. My mood automatically lifted about ten notches.

He was facing away from me when I turned around.

"So?" I asked.

He glanced over his shoulder. "An exchange of information seems fair under these circumstances," he said.

*Another question for the ages: why the hell did he talk like that?*

"In other words, you won't say jack unless I feed you something first."

He nodded. "My body does require occasional sustenance."

"What? That's not what I meant. Ugh." I threw my hands up. "Fine. Whatever. My name's Vic. Five years ago, this rotten scumsucker killed my parents, and I've been looking for him ever since. As a matter of fact, I found him tonight, and I would have killed him if you hadn't shown up."

"Ah." He nodded in understanding. "A quest of *vengeance*."

"Something like that." I sat down in front of the mattress with my legs crossed. "Your turn."

"I know something of revenge," he said almost wistfully. "It never helps."

"Your turn," I repeated pointedly. No way was this guy going to play my therapist. Thankfully, he seemed to get the message.

He stretched out, flexing his fingers, and then stopped short. I watched him pat himself down for something. "My flask," he said. A note of urgency entered his voice. "Where is it?"

That made me anxious. I pawed through the armor laying on the floor behind me. It was on the belt next to where I had found the sword, which was now just a hilt again.

I didn't let myself think about that. Nor did I let myself think about the mysterious golden meteorite that appeared right before this guy showed up in the river.

The flask was ornately carved and small, but it was surprisingly heavy in my hand. I gave it to him. Marcus nodded his thanks. He took a deep draught. "Better. Now, I am ready to speak."

I wasn't focused on his face anymore. The wound in his back had just shrunk, its tendrils receding before my eyes. When I brought my attention back to his features, his hair was unmistakably darker and a bit longer, as well. The lines around his mouth and eyes didn't cut as deeply into his face.

I blinked. The man I had assumed to be at least middle

aged, if not older, had just dropped twenty years in a matter of a few seconds.

"What just happened?" I gestured around my own face. "Here. What just happened here?"

Instead of answering, he simply raised his flask a bit. I stared at it and then stared at him. I found myself at a total loss for words. Maybe the hunt for Rocco had taken a greater toll on me than I thought. Maybe I was finally cracking up.

"Okay," I said. "I mean, *okay*."

He arched his eyebrows. "Are you ready to listen?"

"Yes." I rested my chin in my hand. Maybe his story would help me feel less crazy, and it wasn't like I had cable. "Go for it."

"As you wish," he said. "I will tell you everything."

## 5

"MANY MILLENNIA AGO, it was not just humans who roamed this world. There were gods among you, and monsters, and some who were both. Humanity was enslaved by these gods, used as workhorses and playthings. The toll on human civilization was staggering."

I ran a hand through my hair, fighting the temptation of sleep from the corners of my mind. "Really? That isn't what I learned in Sunday school."

Rather than laughing, Marcus looked confused. "You have most likely learned a world's worth of inaccuracies about the higher beings, but I assure you that your legends are but a shadow of the truth."

He took a second to gather himself, then pressed on. "The gods were insatiable in their lust for power, and impatient in their dealings with one another. A great many wars were fought, won, and lost among them, all in the name of this petty squabbling. Some of them centered around the humans' place in the order of things. So, it is ironic that these conflicts also killed your people by the millions each time. They were treated as cleanses, necessary to refresh the world and renew it for a fresh crop."

"I'm gonna level with you here, dude," I said. "That's screwed up. Sounds like your gods need to reevaluate their priorities."

"You are not the only one who thought this way," he replied. "Eventually, a hero rose up among the gods, defeating them and banishing them to their own kingdom, where he ruled as both king and shepherd. He believed that humanity should be left to their own devices, and that mortal men deserved a chance to weave their own fates independent of the whims of gods or other creatures. From among your ranks, he handpicked the worthiest to help him guard Carcerum so that these banished gods might not escape."

"Okay, first, I was joking. Second, still not clear on this whole Carcerum deal." I stifled a yawn. It was a pretty incredible story so far, but also, totally unbelievable—just another crazy in the NYC. Experience taught me that it was best to just let them wear themselves out, but I was quickly losing the battle against unconsciousness myself.

"Carcerum was designed to be a paradise." Marcus glanced away, looking troubled. "It turned out more like a prison." The corners of his mouth turned suddenly downward. "King Kronin's beliefs were good and just, but they were too idealistic. Those gods who dwelled in darkness resented his rule and forever sought to find a way back to the land of vice and exploitation. The comforts Kronin gave, though they were plentiful, could not satisfy an appetite for cruelty."

"Mhmm. And let me guess, for $29.99 I can buy a book that will explain the rest of the story and show me the true path to happiness and inner healing." My capacity for humoring him was running low.

He eyed me warily. "You need no such book. I know this firsthand, for I am from Carcerum." He spoke without a trace of dishonesty. His eyes and tone were deadly serious. I didn't know what to think. He had to be shitting me, right? Except he sure didn't look like he was.

"*You?*" I sighed. "So you're not just some nutjob who likes late night swims, you're also an angel or something. Explains the armor I guess. But I'm pretty sure I saw this in a movie once, and you're supposed to show me what the world was like if I had never been born."

"I'm not an angel, nor am I a...nutjob—as you say—and I am quite sure your birth and existence has had little impact upon this world. None of that matters to me. I am a warrior. Among those chosen by Kronin to safeguard the palace for all eternity. It was an honor to serve the Hero-King. The greatest of my life."

I grimaced, but sat up a little straighter. "You said 'was.'"

Melancholy shrouded Marcus's face. "I did. Kronin has been killed, and Carcerum is thrown into disarray. I fear that the gods, kept at bay for so long, are now beginning to infiltrate this world anew. Perhaps they have already done so."

"And, what? You're here to stop them?"

I sank back down. Stories of tragedy and loss always aroused my interest. When you're an orphan, you sort of get attuned to that kind of thing. Still, I was way less on board with the rest of his insane story. I couldn't figure out his angle, which meant that either he was totally over the moon or he was trying to outsmart me. I wasn't thrilled by either prospect.

"Yes. But I cannot hope to stop them alone. I have come to find a warrior to answer King Kronin's call."

And there it was. The pitch. What the hell had I gotten myself into here? I did one good deed for the year, and now I had this crock of shit to sort through—on top of everything else that had gone wrong with my life so far. *Great. Good going, Vic. This is just what you needed.*

"Look man, why don't you just give me your pamphlet or whatever and we can say our farewells." I looked toward the door, hoping he would take the hint.

"Kronin was killed," Marcus said patiently. If he *was* getting the hint, he ignored it like a pro. He reminded me of the math tutor I had in high school. That poor kid must have walked me through the order of operations thirty times—but I just couldn't have cared less. "This means the gods have been unleashed. His last words to me were thus: 'Protect my people.' So that is what I intend to do." He leaned forward. "But in order to fulfill my duties, I need the help of a great warrior…"

*Oh, hell no.* Bringing him into my house, that was my mistake. I just *had* to save him from the river. Would-be murderer or no, I still had my morals. But once the guy in Roman armor was inside and on my bed, there was no way not to hear the whole spiel. I made a mental note to learn from this bizarre experience.

"Man, look. I'm sure this king of yours was really great or whatever, but I've got things to do. People to find. A guy to kill. Despite how that makes me sound, I don't think I'm your warrior."

Marcus opened his mouth to respond, then snapped it shut sharply. He stared at me for a second before a smile crept across his face. The smile cracked, and he let out a full body laugh that shook my lamp.

"What?" I demanded. "The hell is so funny?"

"No, no." Marcus held up his hands, stifling the laughter. "You are not the one I'm looking for."

"No?" I paused just long enough for foolish pride to get the better of me. "Why the hell not?"

"Well, because," he waved his hands toward me and then around the room. "Just look at you, and look at…this. You're a mess. I need someone to avenge the greatest being to have ever lived. Someone that can lead humanity in defense against the monsters poised to devour them. I need a warrior, not…you."

My blood heated up a degree. For some reason, this Caesar's Palace washout was able to cut me to the core, and by accident, no less. While he stared down in judgement upon me, I couldn't help thinking of the true failure tonight. It had nothing to do with this man's quest, but my own. The moment came. The one I had dreamed about for years. And instead of doing what I had sworn to do, I balked. I let that slimy rat bastard Rocco Durant slip through my clutches.

He may have been insane and homeless, but he was right. I wasn't a warrior.

I turned and grabbed an unfinished bottle of whiskey and took a long pull. I might have been a failure, but at least I had alcohol.

The soldier in my bed seemed to notice my mood change. He stopped laughing, then held up a hand.

"My apologies. I should not have laughed at your expense. You suffered a great loss tonight by choosing to save me, and for that I am grateful. And as it turns out, I do need your help. But perhaps it would be untoward of me to rely solely on your generosity. Let me propose a trade."

"You mean like you wanted to trade life stories? Or, how about this? I go to sleep, and you get the hell out." I was trying hard to indulge in my natural instinct to be pissed at him, but for some reason, the annoyance wasn't surfacing. There was something bizarrely endearing about the way he seemed so enveloped in his mythos. It had been awhile since I had believed in anything that fully. And besides that, he wasn't budging from the bed. A little smile crept over my lips. "Fine. Let me hear it."

"This place has changed much more than I anticipated in the years of my absence. You may not be a warrior, but I think you would be an excellent guide."

I laughed. "Look, no worries about tonight. As far as I see it, we're even. But I can't get wrapped up in whatever delusion you're selling. I've got my own problems."

"And in return," he continued as if I hadn't interrupted. "I will help you kill your villain."

That made me stop drinking. "And how will you do that?"

"I will teach you to fight."

For a second, my pride got the better of me again. "I *know* how to fight. Did pretty well for myself tonight, as a matter of fact, before you showed up."

Marcus gave a full-bellied laugh. "I'd wager luck carried

you further than skill. Next time, your mark will be waiting for you, and without *proper* training, you will fail. Your temperament is too rash. You speak without thinking. You act without awareness of the consequences."

"Geeze, okay. Thanks for the vote of confidence."

"But you have a good heart. I am grateful that you chose to save me at the cost of your quest. That is a debt I feel obliged to repay."

"Yeah, you're welcome." Then I sighed and shrugged. "I can always kill Rocco another day. I can't bring back the dead." I inhaled sharply as I realized what I'd said. "What about that?" I asked quickly, indicating his injury. "Doesn't look like you can teach anyone to fight right now."

Now it was his turn to puff up his chest. "I was a Centurion soldier in my time, First Cohort. Then I was defender of Carcerum by King Kronin's side. I have honed my discipline over eons, slain all manner of creature."

"I don't know. You really should go to a hospital. Can't have you dropping dead on me."

"My wound is of no concern." Marcus patted the flask resting by his hand. "I have the means to neutralize its progress."

He had an answer for everything I threw at him. I could tell he wouldn't easily accept rejection.

"Tell you what. Let me sleep on it, and I'll get back to you tomorrow. Does that sound good?" Clearly, the guy was deranged, but I *had* seen him mow down those guys at the docks as if they were paper dolls—and he did it without a glowing sword. I almost hated to admit it, but maybe he could teach me a thing or two, and if all he needed in return was someone to show him the sights, well…that wasn't such a bad trade.

He'd get his warrior, or whatever the hell he was looking for. And I'd get Rocco Durant.

But whether or not he agreed, I was going to let it go until morning. My whole head spun with everything I had seen and heard and experienced over the past few hours.

Fortunately, he was accommodating. "I find this arrangement satisfactory." A yawn stretched his mouth wide. "And now, I must rest. Your hospitality is extremely appreciated, Vic."

I hesitated. "You're welcome…again." It surprised me that he remembered my name. I wondered if he'd still know who I was when he woke up. Part of me was still convinced that he was nothing more than a delusional homeless person I had managed to pick up during my little brush with the mob.

Despite my doubts, there were enough oddities about Marcus's mere existence that I had a hard time completely brushing off the things he said. What about the sword, or the thing that had almost fallen on me just before he appeared? Why was he so insistent that the tale he told was real? Who was the warrior he wanted to find?

I had meant to ask him all these questions before we broke for the night, but I didn't have it in me. I gave him a blanket, and he passed out almost immediately on my bed. I retreated into the corner by the minifridge. Moonlight spilled through the single giant window onto the scarred surface of my only table.

Sitting down, I sighed and got back up to rummage in the fridge for a beer. Now that I had the chance to fall asleep, my brain wouldn't shut down. A thousand thoughts rushed through my head at once. Behind my closed eyelids, I saw the mangled bodies of Rocco's three underlings. Killing with a sword felt so different from killing with a gun.

It was much more personal. More intimate.

Did I want that? I didn't know. Instead of trying to figure it out, I threw myself into the bottom of my beer bottle. After that one was gone, I got another. And another. Eventually, the torrent inside my head slowed to two alternating thoughts. *This can't be happening. This isn't true. This can't be happening. This isn't true.* Over and over.

My head fell back on the exposed brick. My eyes dropped closed. At long last, sleep was coming.

*This can't be happening. This isn't true.*

Down into the deep, soft dark.

## 6

A SHARP CRACK jolted me awake from dreams of blood and cold, black water. I gasped, and my nose filled with the acrid stench of smoke. What the hell? I bolted into an upright position, immediately wide awake. Everything from my neck to the soles of my feet hurt, and it took a minute to remember why. Then it all came rushing back.

Rocco Durant. The chase.

The pier. Marcus in the river.

The sword.

None of that explained why my place stunk of smoke. I turned, searching for the source of it and was met with the sight of Marcus tending a small fire in the middle of my loft. I recognized the pieces of one of my chairs feeding the flames.

"Hey!"

He looked up. "Greetings, Vic. How was your rest?"

I frowned extra hard at him to make sure he felt my

displeasure. "Why are you burning my shit? This is a hazard on so many levels! Also, I liked that chair."

Marcus glanced at the fire as if he had no idea what I was talking about. "The fire is for cooking. Was that not apparent?"

"Cooking? Cooking what?" How was this my life now? I saved one weirdo, and *bam*, I was living in a whacked-out sitcom. "You don't need an open fire to cook in here."

"How else am I to do it?" he asked. His consternation was real and profound. He picked up a bundle I hadn't noticed off the floor, and he set about unwrapping it. I heard a muffled sound.

"Wait." I shook my head vigorously. "No. No, no. First of all, where the hell did you get a cat? And secondly, we are not eating it for breakfast. Absolutely not."

"It was wild." Marcus shrugged. "Do you not hunt for your food?"

The cat popped its head out of the bundle. It was devastatingly cute. Unaware of how close it had come to death, it meowed again. I could not believe he'd wanted to eat that.

"It's not wild, dude. It's just a stray. It was probably someone's pet once. Anyway, we don't eat cats or dogs or anything like that. We just go to the store." I grabbed a cup from amid the wreckage of last night's beer, walked to the tub on sore feet, and filled it. The water helped to clear the sludge from my mind. "So, put that damn fire out before I get evicted, will you?" I pointed at the table. "I have a hot plate. We can use that."

"I see." There was some remorse in his eyes as he regarded the cat in his lap. "I would not have captured this animal if I knew it to be a pet."

"I'm sure it was abandoned." I refilled my cup. "But, like, don't do stuff like that. And maybe don't go outside on your own. You don't exactly look like a local." Seeing that it was a hopeless case, I gave up trying to explain. "I'll take care of the food, okay? You stay here. Don't go anywhere. Don't set anything else on fire. And please don't jack my stuff."

Before I could help myself, I cast a longing look at the burned remains of my chair. Then, I shook it off, went behind my makeshift bathroom wall to use the toilet, and braced myself for another day. I had the feeling things were only going to get stranger from here on out. It was not reassuring.

---

I LEFT Marcus and the cat to have some bonding time alone in the loft. I didn't exactly trust him not to somehow cause major property damage by his sheer ignorance, but the idea of bringing him out in public was laughable at best. Drawing enough looks on my own, the last thing I needed was some guy in armor following me around, although maybe it would get the neighborhood creeps to lay off.

I hung around the bottom of the stairwell for a few minutes, listening at the door for any approaching footsteps. Technically, I was paying for the space in the loft, but it was all under the table, and the arrangement might not have been exactly legal, so I did my best to stay on the down-low. Another reason not to be parading a Roman Centurion around right away.

Most of the time, the precautions I took were unnecessary; the only people around were homeless folks, junkies, or both. Some of them were nice. I had a personal favorite. Sam camped out in a little alcove right outside my building's front door, and usually when I passed, he was sleeping under a floppy hat. This time, he peeked out from under the brim and smiled at me.

"Mornin', miss."

I smiled back. In a world where everyone I met looked for ways to take advantage, this man had never done me any wrong at all. It was a small spark of blue in my otherwise gray world. I wished I could return the favor. "Morning, Sam."

"Hope you have a real nice day." He lowered the brim of the hat. I went on my way, but I couldn't get the warmth of his crinkly, salt-and-pepper smile out of my mind. He ought to be meeting his kids at the corner diner for breakfast, not passing the day under a hat on the street.

Alright, look. I'm willing to admit that most of the people I see sitting at curbs or holding signs at bus stations don't inspire much charity in me. If I give them money, there's a good chance they're headed straight to the liquor store. It wouldn't really be helping them. But if I could pick one person to save, it would be Sam, the guy with the floppy hat. Hands down.

Too bad I never had anything to give.

My first stop that morning was at a newsstand, the same one I'd been frequenting since I was a kid. It was run by the same seller, too, a man named Mac who was old twenty years ago. Now, he was ancient, but his face retained its deeply settled kindness. He had always been a

tranquil spot in my life, even during times of the worst
upheaval.

So, I was more than a bit surprised when I walked up to
find some asshole yelling his face off over the counter at
Mac. The asshat was so worked up that spit flew from
his lips.

"You're running a racket here, old man!" he screamed.
"I'm gonna make sure you don't get away with it no more!"
I walked up casually behind him, just another patron
getting in line. He turned to me. "Hey, sweetie, take my
advice. Don't buy shit from this crackpot. He'll rip you
right off as soon as you can say please and thank you!"

I looked past him, made eye contact with Mac. "Oh,
really? I'll keep that in mind." Mollified, the jerk stormed
off in a huff. I stepped up to the counter. "How's it
going, Mac?"

He grinned. "You saw. It's nothing new. Jackasses like
that are a dime a dozen. I'll get ten more of 'em before I
close up for the night, guaranteed." He straightened the
packs of gum arranged on the edge of the counter.

"If it's any consolation, his day is about to get a lot
worse." I held up the guy's wallet in my left hand. He hadn't
felt a thing. "Think of it as karmic balance."

Mac shook his head. He was smiling still, but there was
a tinge of worry in his face. "Thanks, Vic. I mean it, but you
shouldn't be doing things like that, kiddo."

"Don't worry about it. He was decked out in designer
shit. He won't miss his pocket change." I scanned the
display of papers in the front, and my heart almost stopped
when I spotted a tabloid with a grainy photo of something
familiar on the cover. GOLDEN METEORITE, the head-

line bellowed. BREAKING EXCLUSIVE REPORT. I snatched it up and covered it with a copy of the local rag. "How about these today?"

"Glad to see you're putting that mind of yours to good use," Mac sighed as he rang me up.

I put a five in his hand. "Keep the change." I winked as I pocketed the wallet.

"Stay away from trouble, Vic," Mac said.

I laughed. "Why? It won't stay the hell away from me."

The smile fell off my face as soon as I turned away from him. I pulled the local paper out from under my arm and unfolded it, scouring the columns for any mention of bodies found near the river.

My heart pounded. That was more trouble than I'd ever gotten into before, times ten. I was terrified that someone might have recognized me at the bar, or that the driver of the sedan that hit Rocco's goon was someone I knew. I half expected to see myself named explicitly in the article as a suspect.

But the blurb wasn't anything to write home about. There was no mention of me or any woman. Just the usual. "Bodies of Local Mobsters Located by the East River." That was good. Maybe the investigating cops would be paid to stop. I hated to think of myself benefiting from the same negligence and greed that made my parents' case a living nightmare. Still, as long as I was free, it meant I could keep tracking Rocco Durant.

At this point, I'd take what I could get.

I got to the store before I had the chance to look at the tabloid, but I saw it again in the magazine racks in the checkout line. The photo of the "golden meteorite" was indistinct, and it was a lot smaller than it had looked coming down at me. Maybe I was just being paranoid, but now that the parallel had been drawn, it refused to be dismissed.

Images from the night danced in my mind as I stuck the credit card from the stolen wallet into the reader to pay for my groceries. I always felt a pang of guilt when I did that, a relic from my decent upbringing. Stealing was never good, but then again, I had come upon this guy as he was berating Mac for no reason.

Besides, what was the harm? Soon, he'd see charges on his card that he didn't make, he'd call the bank to dispute them, and they'd give him his money back. I had a credit card once. I understood how it worked. In the grand scheme of things, I wasn't doing him any damage at all.

He wasn't special, either. I'd been pickpocketing and raiding purses for at least three years. In my defense, before that, I tried starving, and I much preferred being able to feed myself. Plus, now there was Marcus and, apparently, a cat. Funny how these things happened.

I reflected on the things Marcus had told me as I made my way back toward the loft, my arms full of the paper bag. After a night's rest, his story sounded crazier than ever. Gods? Monsters? A dead king whose protection of Earth was now broken? A magical, gods-only realm? The more I thought about it, the more impossible it seemed. There was no way Marcus could actually be telling the truth.

Right?

"Vic?" The bag of groceries nearly dropped out of my

hands. I stared over the top of it into a pair of painfully familiar blue eyes. "Hey, I thought that was you!"

I gave my old best friend a tight smile as my stomach tied in knots. "Hey, Jules. Long time, no see."

"No kidding." She looked me up and down. "You look a little rough. Have you been getting enough sleep?"

The tight smile turned into a tight laugh. "No, of course not." Mothering me, as usual.

Jules had always been a wine and romcom kind of girl. I could count the number of parties I'd dragged her to on my fingers. It was jarring to see that I could change so much in the last three years of our friendship, and she could stay so much the same. But it did make me feel a little less bad about not keeping up with her life.

"Vic, you need to take better care of yourself. You know I worry about you."

"Yeah. I'm sorry." The guilt crashed over me.

"Really, though. You look like you could use a pick-me-up. Want to stop in that little café around the corner?" She squeezed my arm. "I feel like it's been forever, and I miss you."

That was exactly what I *hadn't* wanted her to say, and I thought she knew it. She always had a way of pushing me outside my comfort zone, encouraging me to try new things or to look at old things in a new way. Which was funny because Jules was a homebody. She never wanted to jump to conclusions or make unnecessary waves.

When it was time to rock the boat, though, Jules Lugnor could rock like nobody's business. That was how she ended up a public defender. She was always looking for ways to work *pro bono*.

A better person than me in every way, it wasn't surprising that we drifted apart.

"I don't have time," I said apologetically. "Not right now."

"Just a few minutes. I'm buying, obviously." She nodded toward the café's storefront, thirty feet behind us. "All you have to do is turn around and walk through that door. I'll even carry your bag."

"Oh, you don't have to do that." There was no way out of this without hurting her feelings, so I pivoted and closed the short distance to the café. What was I so neurotic about anyway? I had nothing to hide from her. She knew every inch of my whole sad story, including the things I had done in the name of vengeance.

Well, not *all* the things.

## 7

A BELL CHIMED as we stepped over the coffeeshop threshold, and a cheerful barista called a greeting from behind the espresso machine. I was uncomfortable out on the street, but in here, I was *way* the hell out of my element. It reminded me of times that might as well have belonged to a different lifetime, a different person. Where was the Vic I had been in high school? In college?

Nowhere.

Too far in to back out now, so I read the menu over the long counter. I didn't pay attention to what Jules ordered, but I chose the drink with the simplest name: flat white. The less syllables for me to say, the better. Jules paid with a shiny new credit card. I escaped to a table in the back. We had to sit away from windows in which Rocco or his men could possibly spot me. Just in case they were looking.

There was no conversation until we were both sitting, our drinks positioned in front of us. Mine had a perfectly circular, foamy dot in the middle. I tried to channel my thoughts through it in the hope that they'd start making more sense. No dice.

*This was a bad idea.*

"I think about you all the time, Vic," Jules said as she poked at her coffee with a stirrer. She dove right in. "You've been through *so* much, and I worry you're going to lose sight of the big picture. Like, what does your future look like to you?"

I shrugged. "A dumpster fire?"

She sighed. "That's kind of what I'm talking about. I don't like to see you not looking at least a little bit ahead."

I scowled into my coffee cup. "That's because it doesn't matter what's ahead if I can't... find out what really happened with my parents." *Decapitate Rocco Durant* was what tried to slip out, but I caught it at the last second.

Something told me Jules would not appreciate my plans for bloody murder. Nor would she understand the scene at the bar last night—especially if she ended up defending me in court. That thought almost made me laugh out loud. In hindsight, I had to admit it was pretty surreal. I was getting used to coming within inches of instant death.

It didn't bother me as much as it probably should have.

"I know." She fiddled with the button on her cuff. "I can't tell you how to live or what to feel, and I promise I don't want to. But it scares me to think of you getting too deep into this stuff. That's all."

"I won't," I lied. "I can manage it. I'm stronger than I look."

"I know. You always have been." She was quiet for a little while. Then she said, "Do you remember that time we knocked the bee's nest out of the eaves of your house, and your mom ran around shutting all the windows in the dead heat of summer?"

The memory was so vivid it was almost physical. I smiled. "Yeah. We thought she was mad, but she was laughing." In my mind's eye, I saw my mother, housedress whirling, hair tied up, slamming the windows down against a furious onslaught of bees. The radiant smile on her face was edged in red lipstick. She made sure we weren't hurt, but she never blamed us. "I miss her."

Jules reached across the table and took my hand. "Me too."

Then the picture of my mom disappeared, replaced by Rocco's scowl. Reminiscing always did this to me. But this time was different.

A golden light shone across his image in my mind.

With everything that happened last night, I felt like I was falling down a rabbit hole I couldn't escape from. Gods, meteors, and magic swords. Jules had always done her best to keep me grounded. Maybe that's what I needed now. I sucked in a deep breath and let it out in a rush. "Jules, do you think I'm crazy?"

She cocked her head to the side. "Who wants to know?"

*The Roman Centurion sitting in my apartment*, I thought.

"I mean, actually *crazy*. Do you think I can tell what's real?"

It took her a long time to answer that. Too long, maybe. At last, she looked me in the eye and said, "You're driven. You're stubborn. You're hyper-focused and sometimes a huge pain in the ass. But no, I don't think you're crazy. Even at the height of your obsession with your parents' murders, I never doubted what you saw or what you told me. I never doubted it was real."

I felt the old wound reopening. "Then why didn't you help me?"

Talk about shit I remembered like it was yesterday. Jules was the first person—fresh out of law school—I had asked for help in locating and prosecuting Rocco Durant.

I had expected her to say yes, no questions asked. She asked a lot of questions, she referred me to a lot of people, but ultimately, she said she wouldn't join me going down that road. At the time, my feelings were more than hurt. I felt betrayed, abandoned by the person I trusted most. From there, the distance only grew between us.

"I tried to help you, Vic, in all the ways I legally could. You wanted me to do things that would've gotten me disbarred if I was caught. You asked me to violate all the protocols I'd just finished learning in law school. You wouldn't go through the proper channels. You wouldn't be patient about all the inevitable red tape. I know it would've been slower, but we would have gotten there in the end, and we would have gotten there without you ending up like…." She gazed at the tabletop, her thought unspoken. "I just couldn't watch you hurt yourself, knowing there was nothing I could do."

Rationally, it was more than fair. Jules was on her way to a law career, and there was a lot on the line for her. She could have lost everything she'd worked for, the same way I did. My friend was right, and I knew it—then and now.

"I should go," I said.

"Yeah. It's been a few minutes, hasn't it?" She got up from her seat and lifted my grocery bag. "Don't forget these." Her eyes caught the top of the bag of cat food I'd tossed in as an afterthought. "Did you get a cat?"

"Uh, sort of. He kind of found me." I shuffled toward the door and let her open it for me. "Thanks."

"So, a stray, huh? I love when that happens." Jules touched my arm lightly. "Remember what I said, Vic. Take care of yourself. You know, you might feel a little less crazy if you spent more time around people. Maybe you could give therapy a go. Worked wonders for me."

"Yeah, right." I rolled my eyes. "Why don't I just open the phone book, call a random number, and tell them about my problems?"

"They're trained professionals," she said. "But, fine. If you won't do that, you should at least come to this thing on Saturday. My friend is throwing it. She's renting out a whole restaurant for the night. It'll be like a house party, except quieter, and hopefully, with less throwing up."

I chuckled wryly. The last thing I wanted right now was to force a smile with a bunch of Jules' overeducated friends.

"I'll think about it," I said in the least convincing tone possible.

Jules frowned a little. "Please do think about it, Vic. You know how much I hate these things." She smiled. "I could use a wingman, like the old days."

I looked back at my oldest friend and grinned."Wing-woman. And... I will. Text me the details?" Jules tapped on her phone as I spouted off the number for the burner in my pocket.

"Sure thing. You better show up. I need my best friend back."

We went our separate ways. I didn't turn back to get a last look at Jules.

———————

I TRUNDLED my bag of groceries down the street toward my loft building, lost in the words that my once-best friend dropped like a grenade between our overpriced coffees. My convictions fought my better judgment, and I knew it would take more than Jules' admonition to break my mission.

But my mental meanderings were cut short when the voice of an oversized man-child cut through the air. It was deep and harsh, with just a hint of a booze-addled slur.

"I don't know, bro," he said to his friend, who wore a shit-eating grin, "it might just be my *hobophobia*, but this piece of filth needs to find a fucking job."

I stopped in my tracks and watched the twenty-something asshats laugh as Sam cowered at their feet, his arms clenched tightly over his chest. The floppy hat, which I always found so endearing, sat next to him on the stoop in front of my building.

"Hobophobia," the other one said, "now that's funny." He looked down at Sam. "Why don't ya go flip burgers so we can get another bum off the streets?"

There's three things I *really* don't like: bad breath, green olives (the black ones are fine), and assholes who get a rise out of picking on the weak. The first two are pretty easy to avoid. Sadly, Brooklyn Heights has its share of idiots getting off on harassing those who can't fight back.

Blood boiling, I dropped the groceries and shot toward

the young jocks. Just as I arrived, bro number one gave Sam a little kick to the ribs, hard enough to make him grunt.

"Hey, taintbreath," I yelled, "why don't you and your friend pick on someone your own size?"

The guy turned, looked down at me, and laughed. "This your boyfriend, honey? Cause if so, why don't you ditch him for a real man?" He glanced at his friend and winked.

When he turned back to me, he was greeted by the hardened knuckles of my right hand connecting with the side of his head. He stumbled back onto the steps, landing on his ass and holding his temple. "The hell, you whore?" He pushed himself to standing and stepped up to me. "I'm going to teach you a—"

Cutting him off, I drove my knee into his groin. As he bent in half, I followed it up with a quick jab, catching the douchebag in the Adam's apple. Before his crumpled mass hit the concrete, I was on his friend.

I grabbed his shirt and rammed his thick frame against the brick wall of my building. His head snapped back with a thud. Wisdom told me to drop it and run, but my short fuse and impatience for assholes won the day.

The dude was tall, way taller than me. So, I pulled him down toward my and spoke slowly. "I'll give you one chance. Pick up your friend and get the hell out of my neighborhood. If I see you again, you won't be walking home." I paused, looking into his wide eyes. "Or...we could always pick up where your friend and I left off."

He shook his head. "No," he muttered weakly.

I gave him one more shove for good measure, and then watched him drag his friend off down the block.

"Remind me not to mess with you," Sam said.

I turned my attention from the assailants and knelt by his side. "You okay, Sam?"

He waved his hand at me. "Nah, I'm fine. Just a hazard of livin' on the streets. Always some kid wants to mess with you." He grabbed his hat and place it back on his head. "But you...you have to be more careful. One of them might have had a knife. Or worse."

I couldn't help but smile at the irony. If only Sam knew the shit I was knee deep in. "Yeah. You're probably right."

Standing, I walked over and grabbed the grocery bag. Just before going inside, I took a sandwich and a bottle of iced tea out of the top of the bag and set them down beside Sam. Again, he lifted it to peek at me from under his floppy hat. The smile lit up his whole face. "God bless you, miss. God bless you. Thank you for this." He glanced at the sandwich. "And for having my back."

"Nothing to it, Sam. We have to look out for each other. And enough with the 'miss' stuff. It's Vic."

"All right," he replied, twisting the plastic top off the iced tea.

My feet and legs complained bitterly about the stairs. I narrowly avoided sending the bag cascading to the floor as the door opened inward. Marcus looked up from where he sat under the window. My knuckles were still stinging from the right hook I landed on that dude's thick skull.

"I was beginning to fear for your safety," he said.

"Sorry. Ran into someone I know." I set the bag down on the table and unloaded its contents piece by piece. I figured it was better not to get into the details on my altercation on the street. "I got eggs, ham, bacon, sausage, bread for toast, and some other things. I figured you're probably a real meat lover, since you were going to eat our little friend there." I pointed toward the cat that nestled in the crook of his elbow, purring audibly. The little fur ball didn't have a care in the world.

"This, Vic, is why I *need* a guide."

"Can't argue there." I switched on the hot plate, put some butter in my one beat-up skillet, and cooked us up a damn good hearty breakfast. The smell of the food began permeating the room. My empty stomach rumbled. Food always alleviated a shit ton of guilt.

I served us both heaping plates and dug into mine without delay. I noticed after a few mouthfuls that Marcus poked at his like a picky kid.

"What's wrong?" I asked. "You don't like eggs?"

"Is this what you typically eat here?" He was doing his best to be polite. It was only half working. "I must have been more spoiled by Carcerum than I thought. The gods' table was constantly laden with the finest fare."

"So, you're saying Earth food tastes like trash because you're used to eating magical feasts?" I had to laugh. "Sorry, man. There's no Garden of Eden here, but there is a fridge, if you don't want that."

He waved me away. "No, no. It would be ungrateful to refuse an offering from a host. And my body could use the extra fuel." He put a forkful into his mouth, chewed, and swallowed. "It is not your fault, Vic."

I laughed again. "It might be a little bit my fault. Sucks that you have to deal with such a downgrade."

I'd made the decision that it would be best to roll with all his eccentricities for now. Even if I wasn't sure what knowledge he possessed or how it might help me, Marcus knew something. If nothing else, he knew how to fight like hell. I could still see the arc of the spear slashing through the dark. And it was plenty obvious he *did* need help. So, until I had more information, it wouldn't hurt to play along, within reason.

But that didn't mean I believed him.

"Hey, Marcus."

He glanced at me. "Yes?"

"I'll be honest with you. I don't know how I feel about all this crazy god bullshit. The only thing I really care about is finding my man and killing him. And I'm getting a strong feeling that something is weird here. But that's all I'm giving you." As I was crumpling up the paper bag, I picked up the tabloid from Mac's stand and handed it to him. "Here, I picked this up while I was out. What do you think?" I paused. Maybe he hadn't seen the meteor; he'd been pretty busy drowning when it hit. If he could believe in a magical god-realm though, I felt confident he could handle a golden space rock.

He examined the cover with the rapt intensity of a historian inspecting the Rosetta Stone. Plainly intrigued, he flipped through the pages. "What is this book?"

"It's the news. Actually, no." I held up the local paper. "This is more like the news. That's just sensationalist garbage."

Marcus closed the tabloid and handed it back to me. "Would you read the most important text out loud, please?"

"You mean the headlines? You want me to read you tabloid headlines?" I held up the regular paper. "Why not from here?"

He frowned. "That one looks uninteresting."

I raised my eyebrows. "If you insist." Most of the tabloid headers were awful. Things like: "Aliens Abduct Woman from Farmhouse Bathtub," or "Florida Doctor Accused of Poisoning Twelve Women with Fake Botox Injections."

Marcus barely understood those anyway.

I flipped the pages until I got to a two-page story about a girl whose body was found in an alleyway without any blood left in it. "The Bloodless Maiden," I read. "Corpse of Young Woman Found Exsanguinated in Dark Alley."

He made me read the details on that one. No blood, no weapon, no obvious signs of trauma. Surprise, surprise, the cops didn't figure out shit. The case, apparently a murder, remained unsolved. Marcus didn't want to hear any headlines after that. He sat immersed in morose silence until I dared to ask him what was up.

"It is beginning," he said.

"What's beginning?"

He turned his eyes to the window. "Phase One."

The ominous tone of his voice made the hairs on my neck stand on end, which was stupid. I wasn't a big fan of the sensation. "I don't know what that means, as per usual."

Marcus took some time to mull things over. When he spoke, each word was measured and deliberate. He had a script in his mind that he was following to the letter. For once, I kept my mouth shut and just listened. For some reason, this time, it seemed important.

"I told you that the gods became locked in Carcerum, away from humanity, because of Kronin, but I did not tell you why."

"When last the gods battled across the earth, they used

all manner of creatures as their pawns. Humans, too. There was no shortage of humans who wished to fight alongside their chosen gods in the war, but there were severe consequences. For a human to fight with a god, he would have to surrender his humanity. Only then could he hope to attain enough power. Kronin thought that this was abhorrent, so he locked the gods away. Now that he has fallen, those gods that wish to do so are recruiting their pawns, building their armies, and making ready for Phase Two."

"And what is Phase Two?"

"War," Marcus said solemnly. "The cost of human life will be in the millions."

My trusty nihilism reared its head. "Why warn us, then? You 'came from Carcerum,' didn't you? So, don't you benefit from this war?"

He gave me a disapproving look. "No one benefits from war. And I am not a god. I am human, like you. I know what is at stake when they return."

"But why would they come back to this place?" In light of everything I'd been through, it was a genuine question. I had trouble seeing real value in my world.

"Better to be king over the earth than an equal in heaven. The gods…are not very fond of one another. They would much prefer to rule, and to rule, they need armies. I cannot say for sure what this will look like, but I know their methods are both cruel and effective. We must be vigilant for signs of a strange nature."

*Oh, no. Hell no.*

Shaking my head, I said, "*You* must be vigilant for signs of a strange nature. I must be vigilant for signs of Rocco Durant."

He raised an eyebrow, a gesture I wasn't aware Roman Centurions could even do. "How am I to know what signs are strange in this place? All things are strange to me here. Whether or not it pleases you, I require your counsel. And you, as previously noted, require mine."

"For what?" I muttered, feeling slightly sulky. This was a much bigger role than I wanted to play.

He shot a glance of disdain toward my makeshift mattress punching bag. "I am going to teach you how to fight. Properly."

I glared. "Uh huh."

The Centurion smiled. "It leaves much to be desired."

## 8

I STOOD in the corner across from Marcus with a rough wooden sword in my hand, hewn from the plank of a pallet. He had one too, and he was showing me how to hold it.

"Like this," he said, gripping the hilt with each hand. "It is very easy. Let your instincts take over, and swing." He brought the fake sword up and down in a chopping motion. The "blade" whistled powerfully through the air.

*Man, this guy is strong.* Shown even minor evidence of his fighting prowess, I felt my respect for him climb a few notches. Sure, he was weird and probably more than a little delusional, but there was no question that the guy could swing a sword.

I imitated him, but it was obvious that I was only going through the motions. My weapon didn't make the same commanding swoosh. The tip of it bounced awkwardly off the floor. It reminded me of getting the blade stuck in the mud during my fight with Rocco's goons.

"No." Marcus stopped me. "It is not yet time for emotions. You must learn the movements first." He gestured downward toward his feet. "Your balance is critical here, especially when utilizing a heavy weapon such as a two-handed sword. One unwise shift could put you at your enemy's mercy. Watch."

He stepped.

I stepped.

He stepped.

I stepped again.

His sword cut underneath my guard and struck me lightly between ankle and shin. My leg lost its purchase. If he had done it faster, I would have fallen for sure. He nodded. "You would be dead, then."

"Helpful," I remarked. Marcus moved his weight to his back foot, twisted his blade, and brought it up along the line of my side, to chin height. I knocked it aside with mine. "I'm guessing I'd be dead then, too."

"Yes." He came at me from the other side.

I stood like a tree, eyes half hooded. The moment our swords touched, I let my arms drop to the sides. "Oops. I'm dead."

He stood back from me, a neutral expression on his face. I waited for him to say something mild and encouraging like he had before, and then go back to fruitlessly attempting to engage me. Instead, he said, "For someone who has built her life around avenging the deaths of her parents, you do not seem to care very much."

"Of course, I care. Just not about this. All those guys have guns, Marcus. Do you know how long this thing would last in a gunfight? Less time than it would take for them to pull the trigger."

"Why should it matter what weapons they have? The weapon is defined by its wielder, not itself," he shot back.

"Okay." I flopped the wooden sword from side to side. "Then, I'm not good at wielding this thing, and I never will be."

"Hand to hand combat has more uses than simply learning to fight with swords." Marcus tapped the impressive musculature of his chest as he spoke. "It hones your reflexes, your strength, your endurance, your focus, your tactics. All of these things are essential, no matter which school of weapon you ultimately choose."

I folded my arms, giving him a taste of my stubbornness.

"Very well," he said. "Let me ask you this. You fought this Rocco when you encountered him, did you not?"

"Yes."

"How many times did you hit him?"

I fidgeted uncomfortably. "Two. Almost."

"And how many times did you try to hit him?"

"Five," I replied, trying to keep my chin up in feigned self-confidence. "We were running for a lot of it. The terrain was difficult."

"Oh?" A ghost of a smile flickered across his face. "May I see the weapon you used?"

My face flushed. "No. I lost it while I was saving you." Which, I reminded myself, hadn't prevented me from going 3-0, in the end. Maybe learning swordplay isn't a bad idea.

"I see. My point remains valid. No matter what the weapon is, your use of it will benefit from hand-to-hand training. And knowing how to use your body will save you in the event that your weapons fail. You must trust me on this."

"I don't trust you on a lot of things," I muttered. "You want to tell me gods are on their way back from space or whatever to take over the world."

"Do you know what else I can tell you?" he asked.

"Ugh. What?"

Marcus's eyes bored through mine. "If you do not train to the best of your ability, then your parents' deaths will have been in vain."

Later, I would understand that it was precisely the reaction he'd been looking for. In the moment, I didn't even consider the idea because I was too busy seething with rage.

"You don't know *shit* about my parents, you ancient bastard," I growled. My hand tightened on the haft of my sword. "So, don't even think about saying a word about them. You don't know why they died, or how they died, or how I felt when they died. I've been through this with everyone else in my life and more. I don't need it from you!"

I hefted the training sword above my head and hacked at Marcus, using the same technique I had used against the goons at the river. The major difference was that Marcus knew how to swordfight, and he was not afraid of my pathetic training stick. He knocked it aside easily.

"It matters not why or how they died. It matters that you refuse to do everything in your power to claim the justice you desperately seek." I roared, charged forward, and swung down again.

He dodged and landed a clean cut across my back. "You know where you would be if this happened."

"I don't care!" I shouted. "You're an *asshole*, Marcus. God or no god."

"Does that mean you would like to fight me?" He blocked another one of my wild, unrefined swings. "I am giving you that chance."

I reared back, coming forward so hard that chips flew off the striking edges of our training blades. As far as I was concerned, it was a real sword, and I was using it to slice at all my hidden pain and fear that I could never be the killer I needed to be to find peace. I lashed out at the fear that I'd choke at the last possible second, and Rocco would somehow inexplicably survive.

I knew in my heart that I couldn't live with myself if that were to happen. I needed to be able to commit the necessary atrocities when the time came. I had reached that point last night, staring down the barrel of my lost revolver at Rocco's wide, rolling eyes.

Then Marcus happened. Because of him, I had to reroute my steely resolve into something completely different. The motivation I'd built to a fever pitch ebbed back to normal levels. Now, I had to worry about whether or not I would ever reach that level again. And whether I'd get that chance again.

Rocco may have slipped up once, but he wasn't likely to do it a second time.

"You cost me this," I told Marcus. "It was you!"

The sword whipped through the air. It was still undisciplined, but there was a ferocity behind it now. The tune it sang was different from his, more savage, but it was singing.

"No, it was not." He blocked me easily every time, without looking like he was putting in any effort at all. "This is good, however. You are gaining in some areas. Try this." He stepped to the side, swept the blade down, and then drove it up and forward with a powerful punch. "Aim it right, and your reward will be instant death." He held his sword against mine. "Try. I will offer appropriate resistance."

I clenched my teeth. Pushing against Marcus's strength felt like rolling a boulder uphill. I put my weight into it, both physical and emotional, and strained with all my might. "Damn... it... to... hell!"

His blade gave way. Mine arced downward. I twisted it in my hands and shoved it upward. It stopped less than an inch from his chest. I was shaking, heart beating in my chest.

"I think we are done for now," he said. "Well done, Vic."

I didn't feel good. The training session left me drained and numb. I washed off behind the poor excuse for a bathroom wall, before slumping on the mattress while Marcus took his turn. It had been a long time since I'd last allowed my feelings to consume me so completely. I thought I was past that. I thought I wasn't doing that anymore.

I was wrong.

Marcus's shadow fell over me as I lay curled up on my bed. I opened my eyes to see him looking down at me.

"How are you?" he asked.

"I don't know. I thought you said it wasn't time for emotions yet."

He sat on the floor by the edge of the mattress. "That was true when I said it. I did not realize how you needed your feelings to unlock the strength you have caged inside of you."

"Don't say that." I pressed my face into the pillow. "It makes me sound crazy."

"That is a problem with your perception, not the words."

I rolled onto my back. "Fine, but I'm gonna say that I still don't see the value in hand-to-hand combat when guns are in the mix."

He chuckled softly. "I have explained this to you. Hand-to-hand training will benefit you no matter what kind of weapon you choose, be it a sword, a spear, or a ridiculous modern gun."

"Guns are not ridiculous." I closed my eyes. "They will mess your shit up for real."

"They can, perhaps, but there are stronger weapons."

"Like what?" I sat up, searching the room for the hilt. I found it and pointed. "Like that?" He followed the angle of my finger. His face tensed up. "What is it?"

Some of my confidence started creeping back in. Marcus could smoke me in sword fighting, but he was no match for my shining conversation skills. I was determined to dig as much information as I could out of him now. It was the least he could do for me after that training session.

And for all the bull he had been shoveling, there really was something about that sword. I assumed it was some sort of advanced, government grade technology. But then why was it in Marcus's hands? Maybe it really was magic.

I shook my head. Next thing you know I'll be running around with a breastplate and helmet.

"You really want to know?" He seemed perplexed by my interest in the sword, and I realized he likely still didn't know I had used it myself. I debated telling him but decided to keep that tidbit a secret. Maybe it would come in handy later.

"Honestly, I really want to take a nap, but I mean, if you're willing to tell me."

"It is called the *Gladius Solis*," he said, his eyes still on the hilt. "It was King Kronin's weapon. He used it to subdue the rest of the gods and lock them away in Carcerum, which was born of its magic."

"What does it do?" I glanced at him. "Besides create idyllic paradise realms, and cut things, presumably." It definitely cut things. That much, I knew for sure.

"I cannot say," Marcus admitted. "I served alongside Kronin for millennia, but I only ever saw him use his sword one time—the night he fell. But the legends call it the most powerful weapon in the universe."

I recalled the image of the bodies by the pier, all of them cut through as easily as paper. "So, it's strong up close maybe, but weapons have come a long, long way since you learned to fight. Isn't it possible it's been surpassed by now? And if it's so strong, how come Kronin lost? He was a king, right?"

"A hero-king."

"Okay, even better."

"Kronin did not fall to a weapon," Marcus said softly.

"He was killed by betrayal. His oldest ally, Lorcan, the god in the shadows, turned on him when he saw a way to bring about the world of which he had always dreamed. Lorcan hates humans, you see. He wishes for a realm with no humanity at all, one in which all humans struggle in the thrall of gods, shedding their spark of humanity to become monsters, one by one."

"Sounds like a nice guy." I imagined a dude with a book of sad poetry in one hand and a journal in the other, dressed all in black. "I suppose you're gonna tell me he's on his way, too?"

"No." Marcus shook his head. "He is already here."

"Oh, right. Because he won."

"In a manner of speaking."

I pulled the blanket up to my chest and hugged my knees beneath it. "I'm sorry if this is disrespectful, Marcus, but I have some doubts about your king." He didn't say anything, but I could feel him watching me. "Why would I want to serve a god who failed at the one thing he set out to do? It's not like things here have been perfect. My parents…maybe they could have used a hero-king by their side, instead of one hiding in the clouds. And then he goes and gets himself murdered. At the end of the day, Kronin wasn't good enough, for himself or for us.. I can't believe in that. And you can't ask me to."

"I pity you and your troubles, but they are nothing compared the ruin the gods will unleash. Carcerum kept you safe for thousands upon thousands of years, Vic," Marcus answered. "Do you know what was holding it together? Kronin. All that time, he was protecting you. When he sent me here with his last breath, he was protecting you even in death. Your troubles that have been caused by your fellow humans, they cannot be attributed to Kronin's inability as a ruler."

I stared at the ceiling. The truth in his words slowly sinking in.

"If you want to avenge your parents, there is one thing you need to learn," he said.

He saw me glance at the wooden swords leaning against the wall in the corner.

"No," he answered my gaze. "Not those. It's up here." He tapped his temple. "For years, you've been pursuing your demons as the pitiable young victim, ravaged by the evil forces of your world. Bad things happened to you. But if you choose to let the hatred of others define you, you will always remain a victim. History has taught me that it is not victims who change the world, but heroes."

*I knew he had a point. If only it were that simple.*

"Yeah, well, you said it yourself. I'm no hero."

## 9

Tea brewed in my one saucepan when the prepaid cell phone I kept for emergencies buzzed its way off the edge of the table. Marcus caught it in his palm before it hit the floor.

"Nice save," I said. He held it for a moment longer, eyeing it with a mix of mistrust and wonderment. I took it from him. "It's a phone. My friend just sent me a text."

"What is a text?"

I flipped the phone around to show him the screen with the address of the restaurant where Jules's friend was hosting the party. "It's a message, see? With words. She wants me to come to a party tonight."

"A festivity?" he asked. "I do not think that is wise. You should not be wandering around without protection. The gods could have agents everywhere."

"Man, could you just cool it with the gods already. I'm losing my freaking my mind."

"Better than losing your head if the gods catch—"

The phone buzzed again

I looked at the address and did some calculations in my head. It wasn't too far from the loft, actually. If I dressed for the weather, I could walk. I still had no desire to chat it up with Jules' friends, but I couldn't stand another moment in this apartment, and Jules could use a wingman. It's what a friend would do, after all.

Maybe the fresh air would do me some good. And maybe so would some company other than a god-peddling weirdo in armor. Jules had said I might feel less crazy if I spent more time with people—preferably ones not wearing amor.

Two hours later, I stood in front of my meager closet, gazing critically at the few items of clothing I owned that weren't threadbare and falling apart. How long had it been since I really, genuinely went shopping for clothes? I frowned, trying to remember.

College?

These days, I only got a new outfit when I had to pretend to be someone I wasn't, like my little charade at Rocco's bar. On nights like that, the clothes were usually ruined by the time I finally got home.

Case in point: the dress and boots I was wearing two nights ago that got dunked in the river. They still hadn't dried out completely, and I had no idea how to get the river smell out of the fabric. Not that I really cared. Those clothes weren't mine. They were just a means to an end.

Tonight, I had no such concerns. I was only going to make an appearance so that Jules would think everything was fine. I wanted to wear something she would like, something that would tell her I was perfectly stable and all my weird behavior yesterday was just a fluke.

If she asked, I'd say I was just stressed out. That was plausible, right? Of course. Communication was a two-way street, and she hadn't been coming my way very often, either. She couldn't claim to know what was going on in my life. Not truly, anyway.

So, I was safe. Throwing on some jeans and a belted sweater, I brushed my hair carefully until all the cowlicks and flyaways from the past few days lay flat.

For good measure, I broke out the makeup kit and did my face up just a little bit, erasing the black circles and bags under my eyes. I added a healthier tint to my cheeks. Mine was the face of a person who wasn't sleeping enough, eating enough, not worrying about everything all the time, and definitely not poking around in the mob's dangerous underbelly.

Once satisfied with my pretense of normalcy, I grabbed my bag off the back of a chair, checked it for phone, keys, and wallet, and made for the door.

"Where are you going?" Marcus asked. He was half reclined on my salvaged sofa with the stuffing poking out of the cushion corners.

"Remember that party I mentioned earlier? There."

He stood up and crossed to me. "Allow me to accompany you to your social obligation. You need the protection, and I am curious to know how humankind has evolved since my time."

"Whoa." I put my hand up. "Hang on, slugger. First, it's not a social obligation, okay? Jules isn't forcing me to show up." That second bit didn't sound wholly convincing. "And second, I really think it would be best if you stayed put. New York City isn't ready for a Roman Centurion in full armor to be walking the streets."

I could already feel the stares.

Marcus considered this. "Then I shall discard my armor for now." I stood in the doorway and watched him take the whole ensemble off, piece by piece, and set it delicately down on the mattress. Underneath, he had only a wool tunic and an undershirt. "I must admit, this arrangement affords much greater range of movement."

"Nope," I sighed, weighing my terrible options. "OK, I still don't want you to come with me, but I also don't want you sitting around here with no pants. Hold on." I dug into the back of my closet where all the miscellaneous items collected. Among them was a canvas pair of painter's pants, speckled with a variety of colors. They were huge on me, so there was a reasonable chance they might fit Marcus. "These will have to do. Put them on."

He did as he was told, but he clearly felt strange about it.

"Yes?" he asked, presenting himself. Still weird, but definitely better.

I laughed. "Whatever. The best thing for you to do would be to stay here and keep out of sight. You've got the cat to keep you company." The cat, who apparently had become mine overnight and still didn't have a name, meowed. "See?"

"The cat is good company, but somewhat lacking in linguistic talents." Marcus caught the door and held it open. "I shall accompany you to this party. Do not fear. I will endeavor to keep myself from looking like a fool in the presence of your associates."

"Thanks," I grumbled. "So kind of you."

He clapped me heartily on the shoulder, and my legs nearly buckled beneath me. "You have nothing to worry about. I am well-versed in the nuances of social functions."

"We'll see about that." Somehow, I didn't quite believe him.

---

THE RESTAURANT WAS A COZY, two-leveled affair with a bar in the back and an outdoor patio. I spotted Jules as we approached. She was dressed boho chic, standing just inside the doors with a group of women I didn't know. Her gaggle made me feel a little underdressed. She saw me, and a smile erupted onto her face. "Vic! You showed up!" She gave me a hug and turned to Marcus. "Who's this guy?"

"Uh, this is my friend Marcus," I told her. "I hope it's okay that he came with me." I was half hoping she'd say no, but her smile got even brighter.

"Oh, sure, it's totally fine! We have lots of space. I told everyone to bring their friends." Her eyes traveled over Marcus's unusual getup. "Wow, I love your tunic! You have such a unique sense of style. Has anyone ever told you that?"

He paused, bemused. "No, they have not, but I am charmed to make your acquaintance."

Jules shot me a look. "Vic, *where* did you find this guy, and why didn't you tell me about him before?"

"He's sort of a... recent acquisition. We're just friends," I added quickly.

"What is he, a museum exhibit?" Jules laughed. "Seriously, though, I have some friends who would go crazy over your fashion sense. Let me introduce you. Vic, do you want to come?"

"I think I'll check out the bar. That's more my style."

It was possibly the lamest thing I'd ever said, but I didn't know how to react to the fact that Marcus, who could be a Roman Centurion, was getting introduced to people my age at a party my friend invited us to. So naturally, I sought immediate refuge in alcohol. If nothing else, I could pretend to be invisible over there.

"I'll join you in a sec," Jules said. She steered Marcus toward a group who looked like they'd just stepped off the campus poster for an art college. I skulked my way over to the bar, head down, praying that no one would notice me. The bartender was a college-aged kid who smiled at me as I slid onto a stool.

"What can I getcha?" he asked.

"I don't know yet," I said, but I said it without the usual acerbic twist in my voice, trying to be on my best behavior for Jules. This kid had a nice smile. Also, when I summoned him, he would bring me booze. That alone made him my ally.

"No problem," he said. "Take your time." Then he backed off, which I also appreciated.

I pulled the cash I'd extracted from the day's stolen wallet out of my purse and thumbed through it. I still had enough to give him a good tip for letting me use the bar the way I wanted—as a buffer zone.

I thought I was safe there. I could sit in relative silence and steal some moments to think about the mess filling my brain. All that shit needed to be run through a mental sieve so I could try to work out my next move.

I had spent enough time sitting alone at bars to know that solitude was too much to hope for. It was always only a matter of time before some prick slid onto the seat next to mine and tried to start a conversation. So, I was ready when I sensed someone flanking me, a well-dressed shape tastefully accented with cologne. He sat down, and I prepared my most caustic barbs without looking his way. I wasn't in the mood to play games with men.

I was barely in the mood to look at a man ever again.

He put his elbows on the bar, and when the bartender sauntered over, he ordered a bourbon on the rocks. The bartender glanced at me as he started to pour.

"Have you made your choice yet, miss?"

"When she does, put it on my tab," the man said.

I was usually pretty good at ignoring unwanted male attention, but this dude's voice drew me toward him like a magnet. It was smooth and low, and it hit a calming frequency in my brain. I had to see if the face matched the voice.

To my chagrin, it matched well.

Our eyes met, and my world shook. It wasn't like a big, traumatic moment, but something about him resettled the sand in my hourglass, and suddenly, things looked slightly different.

He smiled, showing white, even teeth. I was suddenly struck by how much time I'd spent lately in the company of men with poor dental hygiene. Most of the mob grunts looked like they brushed their teeth with a weed-whacker.

"You don't have to buy my drink," I said. "I can get it."

"I'm sure you can, but I'm offering, and somehow, I doubt you'll turn down free booze."

"Had a lot of practice with that one, have you?" I tucked a lock of hair behind my ear and immediately chastised myself for slipping into the flirting zone. Something about his smile just drew one out of me, too. I let myself be grateful. Hell, I took the time to put on some makeup. Otherwise, he'd have caught me looking like a banshee in a sweater.

"Not as much practice as you're thinking." He accepted the bourbon glass, and for the third time, the bartender looked questioningly my way.

"Just a rum and coke," I said, spouting out the first drink order that popped into my head. "Whatever rum you've got is fine."

The kid nodded.

"A fan of the classics, eh?" the man next to me asked.

My new friend was wearing a black blazer over a crisp white button-down and indigo-wash blue jeans. I couldn't see his shoes without craning my head like a creep, but I was willing to bet money that they were leather dress shoes, clean and neatly polished. I got a feel for certain types of men in my self-imposed line of work. I was pretty sure I had his number. All except for that voice.

"I guess you could say that." My drink arrived. I sipped it, and the rum left a gentle spice taste in my mouth. "Come here often?"

He chuckled. "Nah. Drinking at restaurant bars isn't my

thing. It always makes me feel like some kind of salesman." His dark eyes regarded me with an expression I couldn't quite read. "I didn't get your name. I'm Deacon."

*Deacon.* I hadn't heard that one before.

I toyed with the idea of giving him a fake name, but it soured quickly. "Vic," I said. His brows knit just briefly, and I added, "just Vic."

"That's an interesting twist. Guess I was wrong about the classics." He gestured with his glass at the people gathered around the restaurant. "Who do you know in here?"

I scanned the room for Jules, suddenly remembering her promise to join me at the bar. When I saw her, I indicated her general direction with a nod of my head. "Jules." Marcus sat at a round table with four other people, apparently engaged in lively conversation. "And… that guy. He's a new friend."

Deacon cocked his head slightly. "What's he wearing?"

I smirked. "Don't ask."

"Can I ask about something else?"

I glanced at him from the corner of my eye. "If you tread lightly, I'll allow it."

He pretended to think. Then he said, "Are you a Brooklynite?"

"Yep." I bit my tongue before anything else leapt out. "You?"

A slow smile burned across his face. "I started off a little south of here in a place called Dade County. Then, the siren song of Lady Liberty drew me out of the swamp. It's colder up here, but you can't beat the view." He was looking straight at me when he said it. I turned my face demurely away.

"You miss the alligators?" I said.

Deacon laughed. "Don't have to. My folks still get 'em in the backyard in the summer. All I have to do is stop in for a visit."

"How big?" I smiled innocently.

The corner of his mouth turned up. "Real big."

We let the heat simmer between us, sizzling in a few seconds of quiet. The hum of background conversation barely registered in the absence of Deacon's voice. I was starting to feel a pull that I hadn't felt in a long, long time. It was dangerous and magnetic like his voice, but I couldn't deny the attraction.

He broke the silence with the worst question possible. "How about your family? What's the equivalent of gators up here?"

I hesitated for as long as felt safe. The truth came out when I opened my mouth.

"My parents died a few years back. At the same time." I didn't know why I was honest with him, just like I didn't know why I tacked that extra detail onto the end. "They were murdered."

*Damn it to hell.*

Whenever anyone even thought the word 'parents' near me, it was like I completely lost my shit. I just had to keep spitting out the cold, hard facts of my sad life, repeating the words over and over.

*My parents died. My parents died.* This guy was as close to a total stranger as he could get, and now, he knew. *My parents died.*

No wonder I always felt so crazy.

"I'm sorry, Vic." He spoke gently. "I shouldn't have presumed. That's on me."

I gave him a small, bitter smile. "No, it isn't. How often do you expect to exchange funny parental anecdotes with a girl, and she says, 'actually, my parents were murdered'?"

"Not too often, I'll give you that." He watched the TV on the back wall for a moment, seeming to fish for something relevant to say that wasn't awkward. I knew from experience that no choices were perfect, but he came back with a decent one, at least, in my book. "Did they catch who did it?"

I shook my head. "I know who it was, but he went free. Not enough evidence is what they told me."

Deacon's eyes frosted over. "Yeah, that happens a lot in Miami, too. You hear about it on the news all the time. But the families never give up, you know? I mean, I'm sure you know. It's inspiring."

"I haven't given up." I took a drink of my rum and coke. The carbonation helped to clear my head.

"You don't look like a quitter," he said.

I glanced at him, finding his gaze already fixed upon me. Something in it had changed, a subtle adjustment of intensity. Instead of feeling warm, I was kind of uncomfortable, almost like I was being scrutinized.

That warm smile returned to his lips, but my suspicions were already on the rise. Was it weird to ask if they caught my parents' murderer? Not necessarily to me, but then again, I'd been consumed by it for five years. Did he have the right to express such blatant interest?

*Free country.* Still, it didn't sit right. A hidden motive began to form in the back of my mind.

I finished my drink and set the heavy glass down on the bar. "Thanks for buying." I directed my eyes toward the buffet table on the other side of the floor. "Is there anything over there that goes well with rum and coke?"

He grinned. "I'd be happy to check it out. Shall we?"

We walked side by side toward the food. I kept my hands clasped primly in front of me as if my every thought was not consumed by figuring out the best way to pick Deacon's pocket.

## 10

IT WASN'T the money I was after, although he looked wealthy enough. I had plenty of cash tucked safely in my purse. I just needed to see what was inside Deacon's wallet, money or otherwise, because the peculiar angle of his questions had caught on something inside my mental gears. I was worried he might have a badge concealed in his back pocket, and I wouldn't have a chance of getting to it unless we were on our feet.

The buffet table was the perfect excuse.

"Looks good, doesn't it?" Deacon handed me a plate.

I forced myself not to inspect his hands for gun calluses, which I had learned to spot on officers of the law. If I flirted a little more, I might be able to hold his hand. That would be foolproof, but maybe too risky. Until I knew otherwise, the safe thing to do was assume he was a cop.

And a cop—a good one at least—would know when a game was being played.

"Thank you." I pretended to be indecisive about what

food I wanted. It wasn't hard. Eating was the last thing on my mind. I was waiting for more people to come over, maybe form a little crowd around us so I could try and pinpoint the location of Deacon's wallet. I couldn't take it right then, obviously, but I'd feel better if I knew where the target was.

No one came close enough. I picked up a few things and let him lead me to a nearby table. Jules caught my eye on the way and gave me an enthusiastic thumbs-up. A terrible thought crossed my mind. *Had she set me up?* Was the whole party just an elaborate ruse to hook me up with this guy?

Yeah, right. Just my good old-fashioned paranoia taking over again. That might mean I was wrong about Deacon, too, and I was about to make an ass out of myself for no good reason. I'd open that wallet and find his business card as a BMW salesman or something. Of course, if I did it right, I was the only one who would know of my stupidity.

I was determined to do it right.

The tables were small and intimate. Deacon sat across from me. His knee brushed mine under the table cloth. "You know, if you want me to go away, feel free to say so." That smile lit up his whole face. "I know I can be a little persistent when there's something that I want."

I had to admire his confidence. "Bold words from a man I just met, what, twenty minutes ago?"

He checked his silver wristwatch. "Let's say thirty. That gives us a little more history."

I raised my eyebrows at him. "Do you turn the charm up this high for every girl you meet, or am I just lucky?"

"When I have to turn it up like this, I'm the lucky one."

*Damn.* He really didn't miss a beat. I sort of wished we were at a club instead of a rented restaurant. Dance floors made pickpocketing shamefully easy. I didn't even want to keep it. All I needed was a quick glance, or a quick squeeze of his hand. A glimpse at the badge would be better. *C'mon. Give me an opening.*

Another half hour went by. Forty minutes. I was starting to lean toward giving up when Deacon got up from the table. "I'll be right back," he said.

I tracked his path toward the restroom, which went directly by the table where Marcus had been planted since we arrived. It was time to pay my favorite Centurion a visit.

He grinned widely when he saw me. "Hail, Vic! Come be introduced to my new friends."

I went politely around the table as he explained our current living situation.

"Super cool of you to let him couch-surf like that," said a kid in a bow tie and suspenders whose name I had just learned was Ezra. "When I was backpacking cross-country, I met some really rad people, but there were a lot of hard-asses, too. It's like, come on man, I just want to crash on your floor. I'll be gone before you get up in the morning. How hard is that?"

A general murmur of assent went through the circle. I smiled, nodded, and tuned them out. My eyes flicked surreptitiously to the bathrooms. I had to catch Deacon coming out of there. It was the best chance I thought I would get.

He seemed to take forever. My paranoia spoke up: what if he had gone to the bathroom to ditch the party through a window? Not only would I probably never see him again, but he'd tip off his colleagues that he thought I was worth looking into. A girl with two murdered parents was automatically suspicious.

I took a linen napkin off the table and wiped my sweaty palms with it, pretending I had gotten something on my hand. Finally, the door to the men's room swung open, and Deacon emerged. He walked toward our table with his head down, preoccupied with something in his hands.

I kept myself facing straight ahead with a fake smile pasted on my lips, but my stomach did flips as he came closer. He was holding his wallet, folding a handkerchief into the change pocket. *Show it to me, handsome. Show me what I want to see.*

"Oh, Deacon!" To my surprise, it was couch-surfer Ezra who called him over. "Hey, have you met Marcus? I think you'll get a kick out of this guy."

Deacon's body swiveled toward us, and as his right hand lowered, the fold of his wallet drooped down. I had only a split second of unobstructed view, but I saw everything I needed to see. The flash of metal convinced me beyond a doubt. Deacon from Dade County was a cop. And that meant we had to get out of here.

I extricated myself carefully from the table and took my turn heading to the bathroom. The soft, flattering light told me that I still looked good, so no one would suspect a thing if I nabbed Marcus and made up a story about a previous engagement. I could say I got a text, that a friend was in from out of town and wanted to meet up.

Any number of excuses would work, so long as they let

us leave. I hoped that Marcus's newfound popularity wouldn't chuck a wrench into my escape plan.

By the grace of some higher power, Marcus was not engaged in conversation when I emerged from the bathroom. I stepped up to him and laid my hand on his shoulder, squeezing once. He looked up at me, and I quirked an eyebrow. His eyes rolled subtly around the room.

Good. He understood that something was up. We sort of felt like partners in crime, even though I was positive he had no real clue what I was trying to accomplish.

"I got a text from K," I told him in a regular tone of voice. "He wants to meet up. You wanna go?"

It took Marcus a moment to formulate the correct response to that prompt, but he eventually got there. "Yes, if he sent you a… text, then it must be critically important. Let us make haste."

Not quite perfect, but close enough. We put on smiles and said our goodbyes. I saved Jules and Deacon for last.

"Aww, are you leaving?" Jules put her arms around me and squeezed. "Thanks so much for showing up. Fill me in later, okay?" A mischievous little grin popped up, and she leaned in close to me, speaking softly. "I saw you cozying up to Ezra's hot friend. I want all those details."

"There's nothing to tell," I said. "But fine. I'll make up something juicy."

"You out?" Deacon slung his blazer over his shoulder. "Want me to walk you?"

"No, that's okay. I showed up with this guy, remember?" I jerked my thumb at Marcus, who was coming up behind me.

"I assure you, sir, I am all the protection Vic needs."

They shook hands. "A pleasure to make your acquaintance."

"Pleasure's all mine." Deacon shot me a secret look. "That goes for you, too, Vic."

I smiled. Then Marcus strode from the restaurant, clearing a path for me to follow. I didn't relax until the frosted glass doors had shut behind me.

"What news, Vic?" Marcus asked curiously. "You look shaken."

I did my best to wave his concern away. "Not much. It's just, Deacon is a cop. I saw his badge. So, we had to leave."

"Ah. There is not much difference between a cop and a centurion, I will assume." Marcus nodded sagely. "Then we had to depart because of what took place on the night that I arrived."

"Wait, you know about that?" I blurted the question out before I could stop myself.

The centurion gave me a strange look. "You told me yourself of your encounter with this Rocco Durant and of your intentions to kill him. Do you not recall?"

"Oh, right. No, of course, I recall that." I ran my hands through my hair, praying I looked only frazzled instead of scared to death. "That night is still such a blur. I'm still half wondering if it was even real."

"To be truthful, so am I," Marcus remarked, his voice solemn.

"Yeah? Why's that?" I had to resist the urge to look back as we walked away from the building. Maybe Deacon had followed us out and would think it looked suspicious. Or maybe I was just being paranoid. Again. I told myself to take a deep breath and listen to Marcus, who was answering my question.

He gazed up at the murky New York City night sky. "I had never dared to imagine the possibility that Kronin might fall, though I believe he knew what was in store. He was resigned in the last days, as a man might be who had laid eyes upon the future. Now, he is gone, and I am not sure where this new path leads. Perhaps to a hero, or perhaps…" He trailed off, then shook his head. "No matter. We will do what we can with the time we have."

"You're making it sound like this is going to be the end of the world."

"And you make it sound like you would not miss it." He glanced sideways at me, and I looked down.

"This dump?" I asked nonchalantly. "Are you kidding me?" I kicked at a pebble in the street and watched it skitter over the curb and underneath the wheels of some beater coughing up clouds of black exhaust. "Somehow, I don't think I would."

"I am sure your feelings are justified," Marcus said. "But there must still be beauty in it somewhere."

I rolled my eyes. "Not here."

He frowned. "I did notice that the stars appear to be… invisible."

That made me chuckle. We walked in silence for a while, in no particular direction. I was too jumpy to want to head home just yet. I needed to work off some of these nerves somehow, and when he wasn't prattling on about something I didn't understand, Marcus wasn't a bad walking companion. He was imposing enough that the usual pricks on the street might actually leave me alone.

He cleared his throat. "Can I ask you a question?"

I sighed. He was doing so well. But I had nothing else to do, and the edge had fallen off my mood. "Shoot."

He furrowed his brow. "I have no bow or arrows."

*This fucking guy.* "I mean, ask away," I said with a deeper sigh.

"Are there still churches in this version of the world?"

If I'd been drinking something, I would have done a spit-take. "Why? You need to go to confession?"

Part of me decided he had to be for real, or for real delusional. Nobody normal was this dedicated to a character.

He shrugged, plainly unoffended by my reaction. "Your attitude is so secular that I thought perhaps the rituals of worship had fallen by the wayside. This is not true, I take it."

"Oh, buddy." I patted his rock-hard bicep. "Buddy. Pal. There is so much you don't know for some reason. *So* much."

"Would it trouble you to explain? You are my guide after all."

From anyone else, with any other voice coming out of any other face, a question like that might have warranted a punch from me, but Marcus was different somehow. Innocent was a weird word to apply to a grown man, but that was the one that first sprang to mind.

"Okay, look." I drew in my breath. "I don't know why the hell I'm doing this with you, but here goes. We have gods. We have a lot of gods, but they're not the ones you've been talking about, see? They're like Jupiter. And Mars. And Venus." I ran my hand through my hair again, corralling my jumbled thoughts. It had been forever since I'd had to articulate a point on religion, much less in this context. "But the thing that's most important about our gods is this." I stopped, and I made him stop, too. "They're all made up."

He frowned. "What does this mean?"

"It means that man invented gods to make himself feel better about dying someday. Humans need to find meaning or else we get sad. That was like one of the first things we learned about ourselves, ever. Then we learned that making up stories about all-powerful beings allows us to ascribe that meaning to something which can never disappoint us. That's how I see it, anyway." I glanced at him. "Now do you understand why I have trouble just *believing* you about this Carcerum thing?"

Marcus appeared to be deep in thought, and he didn't respond.

"Humans believe in tons of shit that doesn't actually exist. And you know what else? A lot of times, even if you do believe, it doesn't help." My voice dropped to a mutter. "Which has been my personal experience."

He was quiet for a significant period of time. The longer he went without saying anything, the stupider I felt. I didn't even know the guy, and I was out here trying to alienate him for his beliefs while he was still living in my loft. I tried to paint my convictions as simple education, but I was perfectly aware of how all of this sounded.

Then he said, "I am sorry, Vic. I did not realize that these things had painful relevance in your life."

"They don't." I lied. "I just want you to know where I stand."

"And now, I do." He turned to me and extended his hand. "Peace?"

I stared at him, at his hand, and back. "Yeah. Sure."

As annoyed and confused as I was by the current situation, which seemed to be almost entirely his fault, I couldn't help but find Marcus's quirks endearing. He was kind of like a kid—a kid who was eerily well-spoken and jacked as hell for some reason. Clearly, he thought he knew a lot, and he might have, back wherever he was from.

But he had a lot to learn about New York. "Who needs stars when you've got Times Square?" I asked. "C'mon. We're already out, so we might as well have a good time. If you're looking for unusual, I can show you some stuff that'll blow your mind."

## 11

As usual, Times Square was lit up like a technicolor Christmas tree, almost negating the darkness of night. It was raining a little bit as we arrived, and the lights reflected in forming puddles on the pavement. To me, it was the same old garish carnival I'd always known it to be.

To Marcus, it must have been inconceivable.

He craned his neck back and stared upward, open-mouthed and totally oblivious to the rain. Watching him, I realized what a brilliant idea it had been to bring him to the square—he was surrounded by tourists and fellow weirdos on every side. No one gave him more than a passing glance. Not to mention that he doubled as a pretty good path-clearing device.

"This place is astounding," he said to nobody in particular.

I pushed him slowly through the throngs still clogging the sidewalks. An off-tune chorus of taxis honked in the streets. Someone close by reeked of piss and liquor.

"Glad you think so," I answered. "I hate it."

Marcus whirled to stare at me, aghast. "How could you hate it?" He swept an arm out in a grand gesture as if I was obviously just missing the point. "It is marvelous."

I rolled my eyes. "It's a dump, dude. Don't tell me you're not hearing how noisy it is. It never shuts down. The lights never go off. People never stop coming here."

He turned in a circle, half ignoring me. "It is a miracle of engineering."

"And a damn tourist trap." I yanked him out of the way of a stampeding group of people, all wearing those *I Love New York* T-shirts. "Hey, maybe we should get you one of those. You're technically a tourist."

His face lit up. I regretted mentioning it. "That is where we are? New York?"

"Uh, sort of." A geography lesson had not been part of my plan. "We're in New York City right now. This is Times Square, which is in Midtown Manhattan." I pointed. "Over there is Broadway. Over here is Seventh Avenue."

"Is this where the king resides?" he asked.

I smiled slightly. "Not exactly. But some people call it the Center of the Universe." I stretched my arms out and laced my fingers behind my head. "Personally, I think if this is it, then we're all doomed."

"This *is* it." The raw wonder in Marcus's voice had been replaced by a surprisingly fierce determination. "This the place for me to find my hero."

At first, I just looked at him while my brain took its sweet time processing what he had just said. Then I groaned. "Oh, please. Don't come at me with this hero talk right now, man. I thought we were gonna come out here and have some fun. You get to see the city, and I get…"

I trailed off. What *did* I get out of this, other than cheap amusement from seeing Marcus dumbstruck by modern technology? Already, I could feel my decent mood starting to sour at the edges. Would it kill him to drop the hero business for like, ten minutes?

"You do not sound like you want to have fun," he remarked. His eyes were constantly moving now, scanning the sea of faces with impressive, laser-focused intensity. In a matter of seconds, he had transformed from gawking out-of-towner to a man on a serious mission. It was obvious he wouldn't be deterred.

"Maybe I would, if you'd let me," I muttered. I'd made a transformation too: from somewhat begrudging tour guide to sulky teen on a field trip. "Your hero isn't the only thing to see around here. If you can even find him."

Marcus cut a quick glance at me. "Perhaps you would be happier if you were not so negative," he suggested.

My temper flared. I rounded on him, glaring daggers up into his old, maddeningly dignified face. He wasn't even making eye contact. "Seriously, dude? After all the bullshit I've been through, you're gonna tell me to just smile it away?"

He stepped off the curb, and I snapped a hand out to keep him from wandering straight in front of traffic. A cabbie slammed on his horn.

"Hey, you freaks!" he screamed out his window. "Get outta the street!"

"Watch where you're going!" I hissed through clenched teeth. What a great night this was turning out to be. I had to bail on Jules's party because the hottest guy there turned out to be a cop, and now, we were getting abused by cab drivers. It almost made me want to march Marcus right back to the restaurant, so I could take my chances with Deacon.

Almost.

Marcus, for his part, wasn't fazed by the encounter. He was contrite, which I had to admit I appreciated. "Apologies, Vic," he said. "I will be more mindful in the future." He frowned. "I am unused to these horseless chariots, though I marvel at their speed."

"Yeah. They're called cars, and they'll kill the shit out of you."

"To be fair, so would the chariots. Have you ever been kicked by a horse?"

I forced myself not to look at him for fear that I would burst into either tears or laughter. I wasn't sure which.

"You know what?" I said. "I haven't." A great mass of people was beginning to press in around us. It was making me extremely uncomfortable. I pulled my bag in front of me, clutching it closed, and fixed my eyes on the signal over the crosswalk. It turned, and I tugged on Marcus's arm. "Let's go."

Maybe if I kept him moving, he'd stop spouting weird shit every five minutes.

He followed me docilely off the curb. We were jostled by the crowd, and I immediately regretted not putting him in front of me as a human shield. Two-thirds of the way across, I glanced around to find that Marcus was no longer beside or behind me. Still walking, I spun around.

"Marcus!"

He'd stopped in the middle of the road, parting the living current like a log in a stream. Several people looked sideways as they altered their paths to move around him. My voice seemed not to register, so I tried again. "Marcus!" He didn't respond until I was standing on the curb. Then the horns began, and he jogged to catch up. "You can't do that here," I said.

It was as if he hadn't heard me at all. A huge grin stretched across his face, deepening the crinkles at the corners of his slate-blue eyes. "Vic!"

"What?" I placed my hand on his back and shoved him gently forward, mostly to keep him from stopping again. He had gone back to looking up, though now he seemed to be eyeing something in particular.

"I found him!" He pointed. "There. My hero."

It struck me as such an odd turn of phrase that I couldn't say anything for a moment. Then, I followed the direction of his finger—and laughed.

He stared at a billboard the height of a house, one of those that played video. We watched an action-packed trailer play out, complete with guns and explosions and a movie star decked out in SWAT gear, looking cool as he crouched behind rugged cover. In the final shot, he gazed into the middle distance, his face streaked with dirt, blood, and sweat.

"That is *not* your hero," I said as soon as the screen had switched to someone else. "That guy's fake."

"Impossible," Marcus declared. "I must find him. Who is he?"

"You mean that *actor*?" I asked. "Who was *acting*? In that *movie trailer* we just watched?" Marcus was adamant, so I relented. I was learning to pick my battles with him, no matter how stupid they seemed. "Look, his name is Cameron Cruze, but he's paid to do that stuff, okay? None of it is real. It's all made by... machines."

"That is nonsense. I saw him." Marcus scanned our surroundings. "Where is this Cameron Cruze's dwelling? There is no time to waste. The gods are coming. He must fulfill his duty."

"Yeah, you're not listening to me." We passed a bank building, and I pulled him out of the main walkway into an ATM alcove. "We can't go to his house. He's not a hero. He's just some dude." I took a deep breath, hoping that some of this was getting through to him. "All that stuff you saw was super fake. It's like a play, sort of."

He stared at me for so long that I almost thought he understood. Then he roared with laughter. "Ah, Vic! I should have known you would not understand. Such are the trials of the fairer sex."

"Excuse me?" I folded my arms. "You did *not* just say what I think you said."

"It is always a woman who deems a task unmanageable." Marcus still chuckled, shaking his head. "It takes the strength of a man to wrangle the beast into submission. Fear not, fair maiden. We will find Cameron Cruze, for I am here to lead us to victory."

Who the hell did he think he was calling *fair maiden*? I had half a mind to ditch him right there in the middle of Times Square and let him find his own way back to the loft. But even I knew that was a recipe for disaster. I tried to imagine him hailing a cab and quickly gave up. No way.

"Fine." I gestured for him to walk ahead. "Go on. If

you're so set on this, the least I can do is try to help you out." I still thought it was all completely insane, but at this point, what was I going to do? Marcus had no money and no real way of blending in. He had nothing but sheer willpower, and apparently, he was going to find his hero or die trying. So, I decided I might as well tag along for the ride.

Not that we needed to have any more adventures. But besides, he still owed me. And as long as Rocco Durant still had his head, I was stuck with Marcus.

As we headed down the street, Cameron Cruze's chiseled mug appeared again on the billboard. He *did* sort of look like a hero; I had to give Marcus that much credit. A series of dates and times appeared next to his image, along with the words "EAST COAST COMICS CONVENTION".

A wicked thought crossed my mind, and I couldn't help but smile.

"Hey, Marcus." He turned to me questioningly, eyes lingering on Cameron Cruze's face. I nodded at the billboard. "Looks like the hero's gonna be here, after all. What do you say we go meet him tomorrow?"

"Tomorrow?" he asked. Hope rose in his voice. "Is it possible?"

"I think so, although we might have to be there pretty early." Having lived in the city for twenty-eight years, I'd seen the kinds of crowds the convention typically drew, and I was not looking forward to fighting my way through them. But Rocco was out there somewhere, living it up. The thought galled me so much I knew I had no choice but to follow Marcus wherever he went.

We'd made a deal.

"I am honored to have you as my traveling companion," he said with such heartfelt sincerity that I couldn't be too salty about the hell I'd just volunteered to go through. Besides, who knew what we'd find? Maybe the tickets had all sold out already, or maybe they were way too expensive.

We'd find all that out tomorrow. For now, I was more than happy to get the hell out of Times Square.

I TOLD Marcus to wear his armor to the convention; it was the only place that stuff would actually *help* him blend in. He stood with me in the line snaking out the front doors of the Javits Convention Center, and we shuffled forward an inch at a time. It was the first week of October, so it wasn't hot, but the sun glared down at us.

I shoved my hands in the pockets of my patchy sweatshirt. "So, what do you think? Is it as glamorous as you expected?"

Marcus squinted at the doors. "You are certain that he is here?"

"Yes. He's a guest… of honor." I couldn't help adding that last bit just for Marcus's sake. I didn't want to admit it, but the guy was growing on me. Sure, he was idealistic and bullheaded as hell, but so was I. Just in a different way.

"Ah. That is sensible, indeed. And all these others have come to offer him tribute for his deeds." Marcus smiled, pleased with himself for figuring it out.

"I guess you could say that." I ran a hand through my hair and looked around. Ten years ago, I would've been in my element in a place like this, surrounded by people in costumes living out their pop culture dreams. I might have even thought about dressing up.

That version of me seemed so long ago.

Now, I hunched down in my torn-up jeans and ratty hoodie, watching con-goers rubberneck at Marcus and his flawless armor as they walked past. He'd polished it before we left. The shine was bright enough to kill a man. I had to shield my eyes every time I turned toward him.

"Hey, can I get a picture of you?" someone asked. Marcus and I both looked toward the sound of the question, but the kid was obviously not talking to me. He held up his phone, grinning. "Your armor looks sick, bro! How'd you do that? Papercraft?"

"Thank you, friend!" Marcus beamed, but a shadow of confusion crossed his face. "You would like to... get a picture?" He glanced at me for help.

"Not even breaking character, huh? I love it. So badass." The kid put out a hand. "Just stand right there." The phone camera made its distinctive shutter sound. "Awesome. Here, you wanna see?"

He showed us the photo.

Framed like that, standing tall and square against a jarringly modern backdrop, Marcus looked almost cool. Like a relic or something. His armor practically glowed in the picture.

I gave the kid a thumbs-up. "Nice."

"Thanks. You guys are rad!" He flashed one last smile and disappeared.

I looked up at Marcus. "Get ready for that to happen a lot."

It took us an hour to get up to the ticket vendors and less than five minutes for me to drop a hundred and twenty bucks on two one-day passes. It wasn't my money, but we were still going to find ourselves in need of a spontaneous windfall sometime soon. I made a promise to myself not to steal from anyone at the convention unless they acted like a real douchebag.

The guy in the security line looked Marcus up and down. "Man, these costumes get better every year." His eyes fell on the hilt at Marcus's hip, which I had not noticed or expected him to bring. My chest tightened. *Shit.* "That's not a real sword, is it?"

Marcus looked offended. "What? Of course, it—"

I jabbed him discreetly in the side. "It's not. It's just a prop hilt. He'd tell you that if I could get him to stop role-playing for two seconds." I gave the guard a knowing grin. "I think it's the armor that does it to him."

"Right." The guard chuckled and waved us through.

I made Marcus hustle until we were out of earshot. I knew the first thing he said would be something about the security guard.

He did not disappoint. "That man believed me to be wearing a costume?"

I sighed. "Just let it go, Marcus, okay? No one wears this kind of...stuff anymore." I gestured to his whole getup, careful not to refer to it as 'shit.' "Especially not around here."

"But look." He indicated at some guy walking past us in

full bionic future gear, including a shielded helmet and a lighted gun. "Is that not a warrior?"

This discussion hadn't gone well the last time we tried to have it, but I could give him no other answer. "Not a real one." Before he could say anything in response, I pulled him along. "Come on. Let's make a plan. We've only got a day."

The schedule inside our convention goodie bags was an inch thick, packed with fine print and a spreadsheet of events that looked like the subway timetable. I stood off to the side of the bustling crowd, and searched for Cameron Cruze's name while more eager photo seekers flocked to Marcus. A girl dressed in all black, with yellow contacts affixed to her irises, harangued him until he flexed for her selfie. I might have felt sorry for him, but he seemed to be enjoying all the attention.

Maybe it was lonely up in Caledon or wherever the hell he said he'd come from.

Cameron Cruze had a signing and photo op at noon in Hall A. I looked at my phone. We had an hour and a half to kill. I supposed it couldn't hurt to walk the hallowed halls of the biggest comics convention on this side of the country, soak in the atmosphere, and pretend I was someone else for a while.

The last of the giggling picture-takers ran off, and I collected Marcus, who was rubbing at a fingerprint on his shoulder.

"What'd I tell you?" I asked. "You're a regular celebrity. That's modern language for 'famous person.'"

"So it seems." His tone grew strangely wistful. "It reminds me of what I can remember of my original life." A soft smile touched his lips. "Did I tell you that I was quite famous once myself?"

"What? No." So, now he was not only ancient, but he was famous, too? How much more over the top could his story get?

We passed from the walkway into a wide-open atrium encased in glass. I moved behind Marcus, preparing to use him once again as a human cowcatcher. "You see," he was saying, "I was—"

He stopped, and I ran into his back. My forehead bounced off the plate there. "Ow! What the hell are you doing?" He had his eyes locked on something I couldn't see through the swirling mass of human beings. "Not this again. What is it now?"

"I see a creature over there. No doubt sent from the gods."

Before I had time to even think about stopping him, Marcus charged into the crowd.

"Hey!" I shouted after him. "No running! We're not at war, you animal!"

The people in my immediate surroundings laughed.

A guy in a glowing visor tapped me on the shoulder. "You better go get your friend, girl. Looks like he's fixing to pick a fight over there."

"Oh, hell no." *That* was what Marcus had been staring at: a guy as tall and as broad as him, dressed as everyone's favorite space-bound security officer. They were squaring up in the middle of a ring of frothing onlookers. I spotted convention security lurking on the outer edge of the gathering.

This was not happening. The last thing we needed was

to be kicked out of the place before we even got to lay eyes on Cameron Cruze.

I shouldered my way to Marcus, earning my share of dirty looks and not caring about a single one of them. "What do you think you're doing?" I demanded.

Marcus's eyes bored into the cosplayer's, who looked more bewildered than anything. "What's with this dude?" the cosplayer asked me. "Does he really think I'm challenging him to a fight? Because I'm not."

I grimaced. "It's your costume. It's *too* real." I couldn't believe that was a thing I actually had to say. My face flushed crimson, and I laid my hand on Marcus's elbow. "Don't be an idiot," I whispered to him. "Do you want to meet Cameron Cruze or not?"

"I cannot allow this beast to roam free among the multitudes!" Marcus proclaimed. He reached down toward the hilt of his magic sword.

"Whoa, man," the cosplayer said. "Take it down like five notches. I don't know what your deal is, but look." He removed his headpiece, revealing a normal forehead under the characteristic ridged protrusion. "I'm just a guy, all right? Just a guy wearing some funky clothes. Like you. My name's Kevin."

Marcus, clearly flummoxed, seemed to come back to his senses. "Ah, yes," he stammered. "Right." He inclined his head. "I apologize, good citizen Kevin. I was too far into character. I will refrain from this state in the future."

"I appreciate it, my dude." Kevin held out his hand. "Kinda can't blame you, with armor like that."

They shook hands, and Marcus let me lead him away to a chorus of boos from the disappointed spectators.

"These costumes are deceptive," Marcus said. He sounded sheepish, as if he really *did* know he'd gotten carried away. "It is hard for me to discern which of them is a legitimate cause for concern."

"Try none of them," I said. "It's a pretty good rule of thumb. Let's try to grab something to eat. There's still an hour or so before we can go see our friend, the action star."

"Yes." Reminded of his purpose, Marcus stood up straighter and squared his shoulders. "Let us feast."

"You go sit over there, and don't move. I'll handle the food situation." Before leaving him, I grabbed his arm. "I'm serious, Marcus. Don't move. We'll get thrown out if you cause any more trouble."

He nodded gravely. "I will restrain myself. I promise."

"Good. See you in a few."

I bought burgers and fries for us, plus a couple of drinks. When I finally arrived back at the spot where I'd told Marcus to wait, I found him holding a baby in the crook of his arm.

The laughing parents took a snapshot, got their kid back, thanked the Centurion, and brushed by me.

"This has been a very weird day," I said under my breath. "Weird as shit."

Marcus didn't like the hamburger, but for some reason, he loved the soda. "Carcerum would have been greatly improved by the addition of this beverage."

"Not really," I said. "It's pretty bad for you."

He waved me away. "Health is of no concern in the realm of the gods. We feasted like gluttons each night without fail."

"Did you throw it up afterward so you could eat some

more?" It was hardly the best choice of conversation over lunch, but I had long since lost my sense of decorum.

He laughed thunderously. "No, no. Kronin's magic superseded the limitations of the body. Even for humans."

I smirked. "That also explains how and why you can speak such incredible English."

He puffed out his chest. "That talent I acquired naturally. My King chose me not only for my skill with a spear. I studied your language for a previous mission I was sent on—albeit some of the dialect has changed over the last several centuries. Kronin demanded much of me, but he gave so much more in return." His features grew serious. "That is why I must make certain that my sworn obligations are handled properly. It is the only way to honor his greatest of sacrifices."

"Okay." I took a bite of my burger, chewed, and swallowed. "But what happens if you meet your hero, and he doesn't accept?"

"He will," Marcus said. "He must. I will give him no other option."

I sincerely hoped I wouldn't have to find out what he meant by that.

## 13

I WAS GETTING USED to waiting in lines.

The one for Cameron Cruze wound all the way around the hall, doubling and tripling back on itself. Marcus and I were toward the front of the middle, but we marked the very end of the cutoff.

"Sorry, folks!" a security guard told the disgruntled fans at our backs. "This soldier here is gonna be the last one in. Mr. Cruze is on a tight schedule."

I let out my breath in a sigh of relief. If we had been just a few minutes later, this entire trip would have been for nothing. The wallet I'd gotten from the guy at Mac's stand was already considerably lighter, and it was about to get thinner still. Cameron Cruze charged an extra hundred and fifty bucks for a photo.

I hid my frown from Marcus. He didn't need to know what I thought about guys who operated like that.

The line crawled at first, but then its pace picked up. As we got closer, Marcus started to fidget. It was worst when he had a direct line of sight to Cruze; he would stare so hard I swore the actor could feel it. I tried to stop him a couple times, but it didn't matter.

Nothing was going to distract him.

By the time we were two or three people away from the table where Cameron Cruze sat, Hall A was beginning to fill up behind us with the group for the next event. Although I hoped they wouldn't try to rush us, I knew better. We were the last in line, and I was sure Mr. Cruze would be sick of posing.

Suddenly, it was our turn. I stepped up to the table slightly behind Marcus, fumbling for something to say. Cameron Cruze smiled at me. His teeth were blindingly white. They had to be fake.

"Hi there, sweetheart. What's your name?"

That was all it took for me to know how much I didn't like this guy. For Marcus's sake, I faked a return smile. "I'm Vic. My friend's a huge fan of yours."

"Vic, huh?" Cameron arched his eyebrows. "Funny name for such a pretty girl."

I pressed my lips together into a thin line. "Yeah, well—"

Marcus interrupted, his impatience finally getting the best of him. "Cameron Cruze!" he boomed.

I resisted the urge to bury my face in my hands. *Here we go.*

"Uh, yeah, that's me." The movie star looked a little annoyed to be interrupted while he was hitting on me. I, on the other hand, was grateful for the disruption.

"You are the chosen one," Marcus declared.

"I mean, yeah. Chosen to look cool on camera and make

a shit ton of money." Cameron flashed me another grin. He was really going for it. I looked away.

"Chosen to carry the legacy of Kronin, Hero-King of the Gods. Now you must duel me in order to prove your worth."

"What the f—?!" I blurted.

I hadn't known that a duel was part of the deal, and I cursed myself for not questioning Marcus about it further. *Please let this be his version of a joke.*

Somehow, I doubted it.

Cameron Cruze looked at me, at Marcus, and at the nearby security guard. He laughed nervously. "How about we take that picture so you guys can get on out of here? I think the next thing is about to start."

He stood up.

Marcus strode around the table. "No pictures. We must duel. It is part of the sacred contract."

He reached down and drew the sword. I threw my arm across my face as the blade flared into being. Shouting voices filled my ears.

"What the *hell* is that thing? How did he get it past security?"

"Get him out of here, now!"

It was hard to tell if they were talking about Cameron or Marcus. I opened my eyes to see the guard lunging for the sword. Marcus drove his elbow back into the guy's solar plexus, and he instantly collapsed, clutching his chest and wheezing. The other guard caught a stiff arm to the face, which dropped him to the floor out cold.

"Marcus, stop!" I yelled. "Cut it the hell out!"

But Marcus was in his own world, his gaze burning

into his would-be opponent's eyes. Cruze stood frozen behind the table, taking in the glowing sword, the incapacitated guards, and the wave of reinforcements charging into the room. His lower lip trembled. If I hadn't been consumed by a mix of confusion, adrenaline, and panic, I would have cracked up.

Cameron Cruze, hotshot action hero and would-be savior of all humanity, was about to cry like a baby.

He gave me one last fearful glance, eyes glistening and split, sprinting toward a side entrance. I swore I heard him sob a little.

It sort of reminded me of Rocco in the bar, except I had zero desire to chase him. Good riddance.

While I watched the action hero flee, a guard grabbed me by the elbow. It was not a smart decision.

My brief training kicked in and I spun, ripping my elbow free and landing a solid left hook across the man's cheek. He stumbled backwards into a table and crashed to the floor.

"Get on the ground!" Both of us pivoted to face the new surge of guards that had come in behind us. The rest of the giant room was in chaos. Everyone clamored to get an eyeful of the action, but with Cameron Cruze departed, there was only me—and Marcus holding a mythical sword.

"Put down your weapon!"

Marcus did not put it down. The next thing I heard was a distinctive electric clattering. Marcus let out a roar, and then he joined his conquests on the floor.

I knelt of my own volition. It seemed like the most prudent option. Handcuffs were clicked around my wrists, and I was led out by the chain. Marcus was being dragged behind me.

"Nothing to see here, folks," one of the guards said while the others formed a perimeter. "Move along. The next event will proceed as scheduled."

THE FEMALE WING of the holding center was empty except for me and a strung-out girl with wide, staring eyes and jittery limbs. She was clearly hopped up on something, and I didn't care to find out what it was. The cop who escorted me in had the judicious sense not to put me in the same cell as her.

I sat down on the bunk as the cell door slammed shut.

"I'll be back in a minute with an update on your friend," the officer said. She was smirking. "Then you can make your phone call. Okay?"

"Yeah," I muttered. "Fine."

She left. I seethed in silence, gripping the edge of the shitty mattress so hard my knuckles turned white, and glowering a hole in the bare concrete floor. Across the way, the girl with the shakes got up and stumbled over to her bars.

"Hey. Hey, you."

I ground my teeth. I was in no mood to be talking to anyone about anything, much less an addict in her state. But I knew her type as well as I knew any other type on the streets. She was going to be tenacious. In our current location, there'd be no getting rid of her.

"Who, me?" I sat back against the wall and looked at her

with my eyes half shut, making my face a mask of contempt.

"Yeah." She tried to smile, exposing a mouthful of startlingly yellow teeth. "You getting sprung?"

I shrugged. "Probably. Don't know when, though." I had been left hanging before, and with Marcus likely still dazed from his taste of taser shocks, I doubted my policewoman would be back soon.

"Do you think you could bail me out, too? Just say we're friends. Say you know me. They'll buy it."

"They wouldn't buy that shit in a million years," I answered. "And, no. I don't know you. We're not friends."

Little Miss Crackpot giggled quietly. "You're a real hard-ass, you know that? I like it."

"Thanks. I'll say a prayer for you when I get home."

After that, the girl slunk back to her corner and fell into a withdrawal-induced trance. I could practically hear her bones rattling under her skin.

---

"RISE AND SHINE, SLEEPING BEAUTY."

I roused myself from the uneven doze I'd fallen into. I didn't remember falling asleep. It was surprising how much I could ignore under the right circumstances.

I rubbed the sleep from my eyes and blinked at the figures outside my cell door. "How's Marcus?" I asked. "Can I make my call now?"

"He's gonna be a little while." The cop smirked whenever she talked about Marcus. I found myself hoping they weren't giving him too hard a time, wherever he was. "No calls yet. You've got a special visitor."

"What are you talking about?" I frowned. It was unlikely that Jules had already discovered I'd been arrested at a comics convention, and the only other people I knew who would visit me in jail had been dead for five years.

"Sorry," said a voice I recognized instantly. "I have a bad habit of dropping in unannounced."

Deacon St. Clare stepped forward and smiled at me.

I wanted to shrink into the wall. What the hell was he doing here? What did he want? Even as the questions swirled around my head, I had the sinking feeling that I already knew.

Still, I somehow managed to play it as cool as possible. "Oh, hey." My expression sank back into resigned apathy. "Don't worry about it. Nothing about this day has been what I expected."

The female cop made her exit. Deacon pulled a chair up to the bars and sat down. He was wearing a full suit today, minus the tie. The top button of his crisp white shirt was open, allowing me a teasing glimpse of his throat. I forced myself not to look below his jawline.

"Gotta hand it to you, Vic," he began. "I've been working this field a while now, and I've never heard of someone getting hauled out of a comics convention because their buddy pulled a sword on a movie star."

"Ugh." I rolled my eyes. "Can we please not do this right now? I have *not* had a good day."

Deacon nodded sympathetically. "I feel you. Unfortunately, I'm not in a position to make that bad day any better."

I let the air out of my lungs in one big whoosh. "All right. Lay it on me." My whole core tensed with anticipation.

He watched me for a moment with a tiny, secretive smile on his lips. Then he said, "There was a shooting a couple nights ago. In a bar that's a known mob spot." His chin came to rest on his steepled hands. "I've received witness reports identifying the perpetrator as a sexy woman in a tight little dress. High-heeled boots. You know anything about that?"

"A sexy woman you say. And your first thought was to come asking me? I'm flattered."

His smile crept higher, but he didn't say anything.

"Look, it's a big city. What makes you think this mystery woman—who sounds absolutely amazing, by the way—has anything to do with me?"

He leaned in closer to the bars. "The joint belongs to a guy named Rocco Durant. Pretty high up in the criminal scene. A notorious criminal. That name ring a bell for you?"

I didn't say anything, and Deacon continued. "It should. Five years ago, he orchestrated the murder of Ed and Loretta Stratton. I know those names are familiar to you."

"What's your point?" I made sure to keep the edge off my voice, even though what fear I felt was quickly turning to anger.

"All I'm saying is that it would make a lot of sense to me if those two little facts happened to be connected. By one person."

His eyes burned into mine. My cheeks flushed and

tingled. He had me one hundred percent cornered, and he knew it.

I fought back the best I could. "How come it's taken you five years to figure out Rocco Durant was responsible?" I asked bitterly. "No one did shit for me when I needed them to. Maybe if you boys in blue had done your jobs right the first time, we wouldn't both be here now, would we?"

Deacon chuckled. "Be careful what you say, Vic." There was no meanness in his words, but no slackening of his resolve, either. He reached inside his lapel and pulled something out. It dropped open in his hand. I saw the badge before my mind caught up enough to process what was happening.

"The FBI doesn't really go for blue," he said.

*Well, shit.*

---

I GOT up and started pacing the small space. He watched me from his spot on the other side of the bars. He was patient, letting me process.

"So the other night, at the party. That wasn't flirting— that was an interrogation?"

Deacon cocked his head to the side. "Who says it wasn't a little bit of both?"

"But you being there, that wasn't random. You...you infiltrated it to get to me?"

He leaned back, his long legs stretching out before him. "Okay, first off, I didn't infiltrate *anything*. Me and your blonde friend do run in the same circles, although I don't think we had ever met before. But yes, I did go to the party knowing that you were going to be there."

"How?"

He shrugged. "I'm good at my job."

"And your job is to investigate me."

"No." Deacon jumped to his feet and wrapped his hands around the bars. "I need you to know Vic, that it's not you I'm after. It's Durant. I'm going to bring him to justice."

My heart stopped. Five years ago I begged the cops to do something, to do anything. But no one listened. And now, this charming young Fed was standing here before me, my knight in shining armor.

It was too good to be true—and too late.

"Well if you're after Durant, then what are you doing here? Doing with me? Go get the son of a bitch."

"It's not that simple, Vic." He stepped back and picked up where I had left off in the pacing department. "Durant is slimy. I've been putting a case together, but the evidence just isn't conclusive enough. But with your help, I can get what I need to put him away."

"Put him away?" My words were barely a whisper.

"Well, yeah. He needs to pay for his crimes, and I'm aiming to make him do it in a eight-by-ten box just like this one."

"I don't want to put him anywhere that isn't six feet underground," I spat. "Pay for his crimes? He deserves to die. That's the only thing that makes this right."

"Vic, you know it can't go down like that. But work with me, tell me what you know, and we can finish this thing."

I looked down at my hands. "No."

"But—"

"I said no. We've talked enough."

"Vic you don't understand."

I raised my chin and stared daggers back at him. "I'm not saying another word until you get my damned lawyer."

## 14

THERE WAS plenty of time to stew over Deacon as I sat facing the stark concrete wall of my cell. The jig was up between us, and I didn't know how to feel about it. How I wanted to feel was that he had become my enemy, that we were firmly fixed on opposite sides—me vigilante, him a douchebag with a badge—and there was nothing either one of us could do about it. That was the way it had been with the cops and me.

But that wasn't the way things were with Deacon. He cared, I could tell he did. And I didn't understand it at all.

When Jules eventually showed up to bail my ass out, I expected her to be the typical super serious and no-nonsense friend I had come to know. I was ready for her to upbraid me for being an idiot and then follow it up with one of her trademark maternal lectures on thinking about my future and bettering myself.

I braced myself accordingly.

Instead, she gave me a big warm smile as the officer let me out. "Hey, you. How was your stay?"

My brain, thrown completely off balance, stuttered a little. "Uh, it could have been better."

"We'll leave a mint on your pillow next time," the female cop quipped. She furrowed her brow at the sheet in front of her. "Now, is it just you who's out of here, or are you taking your buddy with you?"

This caught Jules's attention. "Your buddy?" She glanced at me. "Oh, you don't mean…"

I grimaced. "Actually, this whole thing is his fault. It's a long story."

She pursed her lips. "I expect to hear it later." A small sigh escaped her lips. "All right. We'll take him, too, if he's ready."

"Trust me, he's ready."

The cop spoke into her radio, and a few minutes later, a door on the other side of the room opened to reveal Marcus. He carried the pieces of his armor heaped in his arms. Understandably, they had not let him keep it in his holding cell. His face was starting to look old and worn again, a fact which did not escape Jules's unimpeachable eye for detail.

"Wow," she whispered to me. "He looks different. And wait. Is he holding a suit of armor?"

I whispered back, "Don't ask."

He carried himself differently, too. Rather than striding, he seemed to shuffle over to us, his shoulders slumped and his eyes downcast. I'd never seen him looking so down-right gloomy before. Whatever anger I had harbored toward him began to evaporate as soon as I saw how miserable he evidently was.

"Are you okay?" I asked him.

He nodded without a word.

---

ONCE WE WERE out on the street, Jules turned to me. "I'm sorry, Vic. I have to get back to work. I kind of cut out on a huge case to get you."

"Aww, you didn't have to do that." I felt a sting of remorse. "You could've let me rot a little while longer."

Jules's smile was pained. "Of course, I couldn't do that. We've been friends for how long?"

"Fourteen years. Almost fifteen." Since freshman year of high school. Jules had been my anchor through a lot of the worst times in my life.

Her smile softened. "See? That's a legacy. You're not going to rot in jail. Plus no one is pressing charges. It seems Mr. Cruze has no desire for any of this to ever see the light of day. Barely took anytime at all."

"Well, I owe you," I said. "Send me an invoice."

She laughed, squeezed my hand, and was gone. For a brief moment, I wondered why she hadn't said anything to Marcus, but then I realized he wasn't as nearby as he should have been. I found him sitting on the curb by the corner, armor heaped up next to him. He didn't look up even when I sat down beside him.

"What's up?" I asked.

It took him a long time to answer, and when he finally

found some words, there weren't very many of them. "I do not understand."

"Talk to me. Maybe I can help."

Surprisingly, I felt sorry for the guy. Maybe he was a weirdo from the way past, the way future, or whatever god-realm he kept talking about, and maybe tracking a theoretical hero down in a totally foreign world was a little outside my sphere of experience, but I knew what it was like to be let down.

"How could he not accept the duel?" Marcus wondered out loud. He obviously didn't expect me to answer, but I let him ask the question. "It is part of the sacred binding words of Carcerum. If the king should fall and the realm be breached, a warrior whose worth is proven in battle shall be selected from the masses."

Okay, so he didn't sound any less crazy now than he had before this whole hero deal became a major issue. But since it had fallen through in such a big way, I thought I might be able to talk some sort of sense into him.

"Marcus, have you thought that maybe you won't find a warrior here? Like, is it possible we just don't make warriors like you anymore?"

"No." He was resolute. "The human spirit is not easily altered or broken. There is a warrior here. I know it."

"Then, could it be that you don't personally have the greatest sense of who that person might actually be?"

He thought deeply about that one for a few minutes. "Yes." His broad shoulders slumped again. "When I fought in the old empire, before my service to Kronin, I took great pride in my ability to select superior soldiers from a throng of hundreds. I suppose not all things can endure the test of time."

I put my hand on his shoulder. "Don't be so hard on yourself. Cameron Cruze does his own stunts. If he weren't such a weenie little asshole, I bet he would make a great hero. So, you weren't that far off."

"Far enough." Nothing could dissuade Marcus's dull mood.

I had just decided to give him his space when I spotted something out of the corner of my eye that made me turn all the way around. My heart jumped into my throat. Frank, the flunky from Rocco's bar, shambled down the sidewalk in a dirty overcoat with his huge hands shoved deep into his pockets. I only caught a glimpse of his profile, but it told me everything I needed to know.

He looked rough. Beat up. Prime for some strategic information gathering.

Marcus wasn't the only one with a mission.

"Stay here," I said to the Roman. "Don't move an inch. I just saw something *real* interesting. I'll be right back."

He didn't acknowledge me at all. I jumped to my feet and pursued Frank along the side of the building, staying barely at a safe range. Like Marcus, Frank seemed oblivious to the world around him. He kept his head down around the next two corners, and then, he ducked through the door of a dive even worse than Rocco's. I wrinkled my nose.

At least Rocco had VIP service in the back. This place looked like it just had cockroaches.

Still, Frank might know something too valuable to lose. So, I went in after him.

The place stunk like a live-in ashtray. A "no smoking" sign was tacked above the dingy bar, but it was so blackened by cigarette smoke that I could barely tell what it said. I made the mistake of breathing in too deeply, coughed, and wiped the stinging soot from my eyes. How did anyone survive in this awful hellhole? Still, I could see silhouettes—presumably living people—through the nasty fog. One of them was Frank.

I was not about to let him get off easy.

He didn't notice me gliding through the smokescreen to arrive beside his table. He was too busy wiping the lip of his water glass. It was sort of reassuring to see that even he knew the bar was grungy as shit.

"Hi, Frankie," I said.

He glared me down with red-lined, bleary eyes. "Aww, get the hell out of here, kid. Didn't you do me wrong enough last time?"

The fact that he recognized me at all was a sign that I might have underestimated him, at least, a bit. I kept that in mind as I leaned over his table, smiling. "Nah. I could have popped you off real easy. I didn't, but I could have."

He scowled. "Next time, maybe you could make the gun barrel taste like chocolate cake. The hell do you want, anyways?"

"I need to know where Rocco is."

"Heh." He inspected the edge of his glass. "And what makes you think I know something like that?"

"You're a big guy, Frank." I gave his generous stomach a friendly pat. "You can hold your own with the big dogs, can't you?"

"Rocco don't talk to me," he replied sourly. "Especially

not after I got my ass handed to me by some fresh whore in fancy shoes." He'd stopped watching me. His guard was down.

I seized the opportunity—literally. My fist clamped down around his family jewels, and Frank's eyes just about fell out of their sockets. He blew out his cheeks like a pufferfish jonesing for a drink of something strong.

"Don't scream," I told him conversationally. "In fact, don't do or say anything except what I ask you to. One false move, and you'll be singing soprano in the church choir." I grabbed the wadded napkin he'd used to clean his glass and stuffed it in his mouth. "There. For good measure."

Beads of sweat stood out on his greasy forehead. He held out for a decent time, but once my fingernails dug in, he cried uncle fast. "Rocco's not here!" He spit out the napkin. "He's not here. He's not anywhere."

"He's gotta be somewhere, Frank." I made my voice as soothing as possible. "Think hard. I'm sure you've got it tucked away in some cranny of your massive brain."

His face turned sulky and resentful. "You're a real rattlesnake, girlie. Them things you say can hurt people."

"The things I *do* can hurt people, too, Frank. And if you call me girlie, or sweetums," I squeezed down harder, "or whore again, I'll hurt you in ways no man can recover from."

He swallowed. "The boss went underground, all right? Jeezum Crow. He went underground, and ain't nobody heard shit from him since then. That's all I can tell you. I swear. No forwarding address."

"You better not be lying, or I'll use that fork as a skewer," I said. As proof of my seriousness, I grabbed it in my other hand.

Frank winced. "That's it, you damned hellion. That's it! The only other thing I know is, there's some new guy skulking around. Don't got a name yet, but the boys are saying he's worse than Rocco. Ten times worse. A hundred times worse."

"Oh?" That was new and interesting. "You seen him?"

"Only once. He don't come out during the day. And he looks like he don't wash his hair, neither. Real scary-like, though. Don't get me wrong. You can't just go screwing with him."

"Who says I'm gonna?"

"Come on, kid. I wasn't born yesterday." Frank brought up a hand and pulled at his shirt collar. "Now let my stones out of your vise-grip, will ya? Hell on wheels. Who taught you how to handle a guy like that?" My face must have been set to mean because he backed off immediately. "Never mind. Forget I said anything."

"You're sure Rocco's gone?" I demanded.

"He's sure as hell out of my reach." Frank adjusted himself and pushed his chair back on its hind legs. He examined me through hooded eyes. "What's it to you?"

"None of your business," I grumbled.

I was upset. How could I have let Rocco Durant slip through my fingers like that, only days after getting closer than I had ever been? The reality of it made my heart hurt.

"Oh, I getcha." Frank nodded sagely. "You and Durant have a score to settle." He picked up the fork and tapped the tines idly against the threadbare tablecloth. "Well, you're right. That's none of my business. But a girl like you wouldn't be in a place like this without one hell of a good reason, eh?" He motioned me closer. "I got an idea. The one time I seen that new guy, he was on his way to the place we just bought in the old meat district. Hasn't been fixed up yet. It's not your grandmother's neighborhood." He glanced around to make sure no one was listening in. "But if I were Rocco Durant, that's where I'd go."

I stared deep into Frank's eyes, searching for any hint of deception and finding none. "Do me a favor and write that down for me, Frankie." Then I turned toward the bartender. "I need your biggest glass, and I need it filled to the brim with ice. It's for my new friend here."

I stood and turned toward the door, palming the slip of paper Frank had scrawled on. Without looking back, I said, "Always a pleasure Frank. See you around."

The sound of his squeak was all the goodbye I needed.

## 15

MARCUS HADN'T LISTENED when I told him to stay put. It wasn't surprising, but I was a little annoyed nonetheless. His shenanigans grew less amusing the longer they dragged on. I was beginning to see this hero thing for what I really suspected it was: pure, unfiltered arrogance.

Who was he to come stomping down from his personal paradise, demanding that someone else rise to meet his needs? The more I thought about it, the more it bothered me.

I finally found him all the way over near my place, standing in front of Mac's newspaper stand. The scene was disappointingly familiar: a grown-ass man making a scene because he couldn't buy a paper. This time, the underlying problem was different. Also, Marcus didn't have a fat wallet for me to pickpocket so that I could feel better about things.

"Mister, I can't sell you a magazine if you don't have

any money," Mac said, shrugging. "Then I'd just be giving them away, and I can't afford to do that."

"And you would refuse my offer of a trade?" Marcus asked incredulously.

Mac chuckled. "The barter system's a long way gone, pal. These days, it's money or nothing."

I pinched the bridge of my nose. *This cannot be happening to me.* Gathering my resolve, I marched up behind Marcus and tapped him on the shoulder. "Hey, Wonder Tunic. What's going on here?"

"I merely wished to exchange with this gentleman for a book, yet he will not allow it!" Marcus spoke with genuine outrage, gesturing broadly at the little stand.

"Right, because like he said, you don't have money." I fished the formerly fat wallet out of my purse. "Lucky for you, I happen to have some." I put a dollar on the counter. "Just the magazine for him. Keep the change. Consider it an inconvenience fee." Mac raised his bushy eyebrows at me, and I shook my head. "Come on, Marcus. Let's get home before this shitty day slides any further into the dumps." I led him away and glanced at the periodical in his hand. "Why'd you want that so bad, anyway?"

He displayed the cover proudly. "Behold! I have found a new hero."

I rolled my eyes so hard they nearly fell out of my skull. "Okay, first of all, that is *not* a hero. That is a guy who stars in yogurt commercials for middle-aged women. Second, did you learn nothing from today? Nothing at all?"

"All failure is but a minor setback and must simply be overcome." Marcus would not take his gaze away from the magazine cover. "We must find this warrior at once. Much time has been lost to other pursuits."

"Yeah, pursuits that happened because of you." I'd had it with his bullshit. I was not about to go traipsing all over New York in search of a handsome sitcom actor turned yogurt spokesperson. He could be in California, for all I knew. Or Florida. Or literally anywhere. "I think we've done more than enough of your stuff for one day. It's time for you to help me. I've got a lead. It's a warehouse in the Meatpacking District."

Marcus shook his head. "I cannot be distracted. More now than ever I need to be true to my course. The true hero is out there, waiting for me to find him."

I clenched my fists. "There are no heroes, man! We're all just miserable people trying to make our way in a shitty world. We don't care about gods or war or that swanky golden place you used to live in. We just want to survive!" I glared at him. "Or maybe you forgot that's what *my* quest is about. Survival and vengeance. Real shit. Not some mythical donkey piss about heroes."

"If you want to continue in your unbelief, that is your choice," Marcus told me, his voice unwavering. "My quest for a warrior sits above all else."

That was enough for me. I got right up in his face, standing so that he couldn't walk any further without bowling me over. "I will continue in my unbelief. And you can keep chasing down your damned hero. But next time you get thrown behind bars, just remember that it was your belief that got you there."

I spun on my heel and stormed off down the street, fuming. It didn't sound like he was following, nor did he call out to me as I left. Whatever. I had far more important things to think about at the moment, like the address I had gotten from Frank before leaving the bar.

I headed for the nearest bus stop, reaching into my purse. There was the wallet, there was my phone, and there was a certain sword hilt.

Marcus had never even felt it disappear.

His ranting about the gods might be bullshit, but this sword had some serious stopping power. And I was not about to turn down the opportunity to run Durant through with it.

I took up my post by the bus stop marker.

Next stop: sweet revenge.

———

THE BUS RUMBLED down Horatio Street at the southern border of the Meatpacking District, pitching and weaving with the driver's lead foot. There were open seats, but I stood above the stairs leading out the back door. I was way too wired to sit. The address Frank had given me burned in my eyes even when I closed them.

I couldn't stop thinking, *I should have known.*

Which was absolutely, one hundred percent crazy. Despite all the legwork I'd done over the past five years, it was still a crapshoot every time. I had to be careful, or else the assholes might start to recognize me. Yeah, I knew my way around the mob scene better than I ever thought I would, but each scrap of the puzzle had a lot of luck mixed in. Too much, maybe.

I'd gotten this far because I was smart and because I had

talked to, punched, and hunted down the right people. If they were all instructed to keep the new place hush-hush, then they weren't going to tell the nosy broad poking around in places she didn't belong. As soon as Frank mentioned the Meatpacking District, though, things sort of clicked in my head.

Really, where else would the pricks run off to? An old slaughterhouse seemed more or less like Rocco Durant's natural habitat. I shoved my hands deep in the pockets of my sweatshirt and glowered at my shoes. A robotic female voice announced the next stop.

Mine.

Nobody looked up as I stepped off the bus. I turned left and walked a block. The building was a brick-fronted hulk, long, squat, and ugly as sin. A couple of its windows were broken, and in places, the façade had begun to crumble. When Frank said new, evidently, he meant it. Rocco Durant never let dumps stay dumps for long. In a month, this place would be cleaned up, a blank slate.

Good thing I was here early.

Three doors—right, left, and center—lined the ground floor. The double set in the middle had a huge, heavy padlock on a boat chain looped through the handles. So, that was out. Even if I could figure out how to pick that thing, with my luck, it would break my foot when it hit the ground. I turned my attention to the sides.

The right was guarded by a couple of roided-up meat-heads, their eyes shielded by giant, reflective sunglasses. They looked like wax figures standing there in the shadow of the overhang with their arms crossed in front of them.

One of them held a serious-looking gun. It was currently pointed down at the ground.

I sure as hell didn't want it pointed at me.

It was hard to tell where Thing One and Thing Two were looking on account of the sunglasses. Their inhumanly chiseled faces pointed away from me for the moment, so I continued strolling casually along the sidewalk, pretending to mind my own business. I had the distinct feeling that lingering too long would be a death sentence.

Fortunately, the guards on the left were hardly as attentive as their gym-bro counterparts. In fact, they barely looked old enough to drink, let alone to be hanging around an abandoned slaughterhouse that had been recently purchased by the mob.

I watched them trade hits from a hand-rolled cigarette with a telltale skunky smell. They took their eyes off their phone screens maybe once a minute.

Perfect time for a little recon.

They didn't see me slide into the alley running adjacent to the building. I picked my way through a minefield of trash bags, trying not to think about how much time I'd spent in alleys lately. I wished I had thought to bring something to cover my face. I wasn't worried about being recognized for once, but the smell could have peeled paint.

The passage was littered with more garbage and general debris, but it was otherwise unguarded. It ended at a short wall, which I hopped over, and I found myself in a narrow courtyard lined with dumpsters. I ducked through a cloud of flies, grimacing.

"Nice place you got here, Rocco," I muttered.

Around the corner, the space opened up into a series of loading docks. My breath caught in my throat, and I ducked down behind one of the dumpsters. The area was deserted, but movement caught my eye up in the bank of dirty windows on the second floor.

I squinted. The mask of dust made it hard to identify the figure standing with his back to the sill. Then, he made a half turn toward me, and I knew who it was.

Rocco Durant.

*That son of a bitch.* I balled my hand into a fist and beat it against my thigh. As if he was hanging out in an abandoned building *just* to spite me. As if I hadn't shown up specifically looking for him.

All I wanted to do was turn around and haul ass inside, but this time, I managed to exercise restraint. I pressed the heels of my hands against my eyes and let out a pained groan. Once again, I had rushed in unprepared.

Rocco was right in front of me, and I didn't even have my gun or *any* proper weapon. All I had was Marcus's sword, and who knew if that would come through for me again? What seemed like a great idea twenty minutes ago now seemed delusional. I could barely wield my training sword, let alone go up against trained guards. And what if I couldn't get the sword to work? Maybe it had rules or some shit, like it wouldn't activate unless I was in a life or death situation. I didn't know.

And I couldn't risk it.

I slunk back toward Dumpster Alley, steeling my senses against the onslaught of rancid fumes. My eyes kept darting back toward the window with Rocco Durant in it, but by the second or third glance, he was gone.

Something other than my customary burning hatred of him was nagging at me, and it wasn't until I was back on the street that I figured out the problem.

I had shot him. I *knew* I had shot him. Twice. The last time I saw him, he was bloody and looked like shit.

Not anymore.

He looked fine. Better than fine. He looked like he'd stepped into a time machine set for ten years ago.

I wiped the intense frown off my face as I ambled down toward the end of the block. On my way across the street, I spotted a car pulling up to the curb, depositing a couple of suits with girls on their arms. I only caught a glimpse of them before they headed toward the door on the right, but it didn't take a genius to work out what they were going to do. A sour taste filled my mouth as I pulled open the door of the bodega on the corner.

I didn't want to let Rocco's building out of my sight, but there was no good place to hide, and I couldn't just double back immediately. I had to waste some time.

Twenty minutes later, I left the store with a dollar coffee in my hand, giving the fat tabby perched in the front window a farewell scratch behind the ears. It seemed prudent to stay on the opposite side of the street from Rocco's building as I made my way toward it, so I looked as inconspicuous as possible. I stared straight ahead, but all my attention was focused in my peripheral vision.

No sign of the goons who'd brought in their girls. No sign of Rocco, either.

The guards at each door hadn't budged.

I had drawn almost even with them on the left when I heard the scream.

## 16

IT WAS UNMISTAKABLE, a silence-shattering shriek that cut through the broken window panes like a laser. It was a scream of pain and terror. I froze and then turned to stare at the worn brick façade before I could help myself. One of the guards jumped, but the other didn't even look up. My gaze danced from window to window, trying to pick out the source of the scream.

Now, it seemed like that layer of grime served a purpose.

I gritted my teeth. The sword hilt felt like an iron weight in my bag. It still wasn't my gun, but it was better than nothing. And clearly, whatever was happening inside Rocco Durant's new digs, those girls were *not* enjoying it. The situation was now or never.

I booked it across the street without looking for traffic. Those two shitty men never saw me coming. I pushed the first one into the wall, hard enough that he crumpled up, gasping for air.

"Hey!" said the other one. "*Hey!* What the hell are you doing, lady?"

Up close, I saw that I'd been right about his age. Only the finest of facial hairs graced his scraggly chin, and his cheeks were a warzone of acne. No way could I kill him, but I could knock him out guilt-free.

"Sorry, bud," I said.

He had approximately half a second to look confused before I hit him square in the head with the butt of the sword. His backward-turned cap slipped sideways as he fell.

I stepped over his unconscious body. Without a doubt, there were already cameras everywhere; surveillance was always Rocco's first priority. It was how he'd always stayed a step ahead of me, even when I managed to get the drop on him. He'd know I was there soon enough.

And I'd already beaten on two teenaged guards, so I was fully committed to this little adventure.

I glanced behind me as I reached for the doorknob. When I turned back, my face collapsed in an expression of total dismay. Instead of a handle, the door had a keypad recessed into the metal.

"Codes," I whispered. "Why didn't I think of codes?"

Just for shits and giggles, I punched a few numbers into the display. My reward was a loud, accusatory beep. Maybe not the smartest idea.

I sighed, tightened my grip on Marcus's sword, which remained bladeless, and got ready to bash the everloving hell out of the keypad. It was way too late to back out now. With any luck, I could brute force my way through the locking mechanism.

The sound of another car interrupted my downward swing. I nearly smacked myself in the face with that damn hilt as I spun around out of pure instinct to see who was coming up behind me. This car was black, too, but much nicer than the first. A luxury car, probably foreign, with its windows all blacked out.

The door opened.

I caught a glimpse of a shoe and the bottom of a black duster. Then, my eye seemed to snap right to a gaunt, sallow face. He had long, dark hair, parted in the middle with comb tracks still visible along his lean skull.

He was staring right at me.

I panicked. Why couldn't I do anything? Why couldn't I move? My feet might as well have been rooted to the ground. His huge, eerily pale eyes floated up toward the sword still raised in my hand, and a ghost of some emotion swarmed over his face. His own hand began to lift from his side.

Why hadn't he said anything yet?

"Vic!"

Both of us, me and the creep in the duster, turned toward that familiar voice. Marcus charged down the middle of the street like a bull, armored up with a spear in hand. He cocked his arm and threw it so hard I heard the point whistling through the air.

The stranger's hair flipped back at his ear as he leapt out of the way. Marcus's spear embedded itself in the fancy car with a screaming crunch of metal. Stunned, I stared at its shaft, still vibrating as it protruded from the wrecked chassis.

Marcus reached me a second later. For an old guy, he

could run like hell. He seized me around the waist and started to drag me away. I realized my quest for vengeance was about to be thwarted for the second time in a week, and both times were Marcus's fault.

If he was so set on a war, I'd give him one.

"Let me go!" I screeched as fiercely as I could. I pushed and scratched at the arm he had locked around me, but even my sharp, ragged nails had no effect on his gauntlets. "He's in there! Do you hear me? He's *in* there!"

My protests fell on deaf ears, so I twisted around in order to shout in Marcus's face better. I saw that his eyes were dark, and his mouth was set in a grim line. If I hadn't been so unbelievably pissed, I might have been worried, but I *was* unbelievably pissed, so worry fell to the wayside.

"Put me down, asshole! Put me *down*!"

As a last resort, I went dead limp, hoping the task of carting my body around would prove more frustrating than it was worth.

Marcus was undeterred. He paused to adjust his grip, and then, he just kept trucking. I could scream and cry and swear at him all damn day, as far as he was concerned. We were getting out of there.

I stopped fighting eventually, and after about a half mile, he let me go. I shoved away from him with all the force and petulance of a scorned lover, making sure my displeasure was written all over my face.

He didn't look at me, but as he dusted off his hands and pulled ahead, he said, "There are many things you do not understand, Vic." A short pause. "I have just saved your life."

Of all the wrong things in the world to say, that was pretty close to the top of the list. I folded my arms. "Oh, please. Tell me all about how you rescued me from those punks who were drooling on the ground when you showed up."

He drew his brows down in a gesture of obvious exasperation that I found extremely satisfying. "I am not referring to those boys you so judiciously dispatched with my sword."

"What, you mean the toothpick in the coat?" I downplayed the effect that strange guy had just had on me for bravado's sake. I didn't want Marcus to know he had stopped me with nothing more than a stare from those paralyzing eyes. In fact, I didn't even want to think about that. It made me severely uncomfortable to know some scrawny nerd had effectively disarmed me without a weapon of his own.

Marcus sighed. "As I said, you do not understand." His tone was long-suffering, like I was the one trying his patience. Yet another thing that pissed me off.

"Whatever," I said. "Apparently, I don't understand anything."

He glanced at me. I wasn't even close to looking at him, but I felt it. "Apparently, you do not, despite how I have tried to warn you. This world—your world—is no longer what it once was. The gods have arrived, and you have stared one in the face."

WE WALKED the three and a half remaining miles back to Brooklyn Heights in silence, each of us embroiled in our own thoughts. I kept my gaze stubbornly averted, lest he try to strike up another conversation. The last thing I wanted to do was talk to Marcus after he'd robbed me of my ultimate goal yet again.

The first time, I could tell myself it wasn't his fault. This time, I wasn't feeling quite so charitable. What pissed me off the most is that I had done exactly what he suggested. I'd went in, zero victim and all hero, and he pulled me the hell out.

I let the door slam shut behind me, and the loft's windows rattled. Marcus went over and installed himself at the table, and I slouched my way to the bed. For several more minutes, we gave each other the silent treatment. I knew he was waiting for me to break under the pressure of not knowing anything, and I didn't want to give him the satisfaction.

But I was only human. I couldn't stand it forever.

"So, are you going to explain or not?" I kept my back to him, staring a hole in the wall. "How I stared a god in the face?"

Marcus shifted in his chair. His armor clanked jarringly. All of a sudden, he seemed reluctant to fill me in. "Where shall I begin?" he asked.

"Anywhere you want. I couldn't care less." I laid back on the mattress and closed my eyes, but the image of the guy in the duster appeared behind my eyelids with unsettling clarity. I felt almost like he could still see me. I settled for counting the hairline cracks in the ceiling.

Marcus hemmed and hawed a little while longer. I

waited as patiently as possible, but my fuse was running short. He had dicked me around a hell of a lot with all his talk about supernatural bullshit, and I was determined to get to the bottom of it since he was so determined to stick around. If he was a crazy vagrant after all, I had a right to know.

"Technically, the man in the metal chariot was a demigod," he said at last.

*Great.*

"Here we go again," I retorted. "Dude, enough with this stuff about gods, okay? We all went to church as kids, and we all rebelled against it when we were teenagers. We did not all invent some insane other world where mythology is real." It was the nicest I could possibly be, considering how worn out and frazzled I felt. "Just drop it already. Why are you really here?"

He didn't say anything for at least five minutes. When he spoke again, his voice was low and tough, unlike anything I'd heard from him before. "Perhaps I was wrong about you, Vic. I thought you were determined, resilient, and possessed of an inner strength that was admirable, if misguided.

"But you are weak. You are too consumed with your untenable notions of vengeance to focus on what really matters." His chair scraped against the floor as he rose to his feet. "Days ago, I told you that revenge never helps. I vowed to teach you. Now, I see that you have learned *nothing.*"

I sat bolt upright on the mattress, glaring daggers at him. The day's emotions welling up inside of me. "You don't know the first thing about me, you delusional prick."

My voice dripped with venom that I hoped was enough to conceal the harsh sting of his words. I stood up from the bed. "You think I haven't learned anything, huh? We'll see about that."

I snatched my training sword off the floor and charged him.

## 17

I HEAVED the sword back and let out a cry full of anger, fear, sadness, and regret. The dull wooden blade chopped through the air and was met by Marcus's expert counter, raining chips down onto the floor. He had a perfect answer for every erratic movement I threw at him, even when I was certain there was no way for him to predict my wild flailing. The heavy *thock* of our sparring resonated in my body, thrumming down through my feet into the floor.

I struck out again and again. Marcus blocked again and again. He maneuvered around me on nimble feet, his eyes never leaving my chopping blade. I managed, through trial, error, and a bit of dumb luck, to weasel him back toward a corner of the apartment where my sad, makeshift punching bag still stood.

Marcus bumped his elbow against it.

Though minor, the collision threw him off enough that in order to regain his balance, he was forced to leave his side exposed. Seizing the opportunity, I lunged forward and brought my weapon solidly into what would have been his ribcage if he hadn't twisted away at the last moment. The wooden sword bit into the edge of his back.

I let out a yell of triumph.

Instead of swiveling toward me with a swift, decisive counter, Marcus fell to a knee.

I gasped. He grunted, shielding the spot where I had hit him. Too late, I recalled the black wound he had when I found him. All the anger fled my system in favor of remorse. I couldn't tell which felt worse.

"Oh, shit," I said. "Are you okay?"

He gestured vaguely in the direction of the table. "Flask. My flask."

"Right." I swiped it from the table, opened the top, and handed it to him. I could have sworn it had been *much* heavier the last time I held it.

He took a long draught. "Thanks." Almost instantly, the color bled back into his skin. His hair darkened, its threads of silver disappearing. Marcus straightened and then let himself sit heavily back.

"Better?" I asked, somewhat sheepishly.

"Better."

"The flask feels light," I said. Vic Stratton, champion of unhelpfulness. He waved me off, and I plopped down beside him. "I'm sorry. I wasn't thinking."

"Worry not, Vic." A slight smile eased the severity of his features. "It just proves that I am at least not a worthless pedagogue." He patted me gently on the shoulder. "I owe you an apology as well. Anger is no excuse for the hurtful barbs I have thrown."

I nodded. "Hurtful, but more or less correct. I've got a lot to work on."

It didn't feel so bad admitting that to him now. The monster of rage and pain had been safely locked away.

"If it helps, I was wrong about being wrong. You are strong, you are determined, and you are certainly resilient. That is admirable."

A lump threatened to form in my throat. "Thanks, man." I rubbed my face to keep any tears from getting the wrong idea. "Thanks, Marcus."

His smile widened. "It is an honor to put up with you, Vic."

We laughed. It felt good. Great, even.

"I'm glad that stuff makes you feel better, whatever it is," I said.

"As am I." He fell silent then, thinking deeply. "There is one more thing for which I must offer my penitence."

"Just one?" My grin made it clear I was joking.

"No matter what my personal feelings on the matter are, it is not my place to interfere with your mission against these foes. However, it would have been disastrous had you been killed and the *Gladius Solis* taken by the wrong hands. This is the reasoning I should have offered at the outset. I was erroneous in believing you would not understand. The sword is more important than me—more important than anything."

I nodded, but said nothing as we lapsed into another silence. Then I said, "Did you find the yogurt commercial guy?"

He snorted. "I think my quest to find a hero will have to wait. There are more immediate concerns that require my attention. The injustices befalling our two worlds have intersected at last. Perhaps in vanquishing your nemesis and learning of the gods' new scheme on Earth, I will find my hero."

I raised my eyebrows. "Does this have something to do with the guy at the slaughterhouse?"

Marcus paused. "Why do you call it that?" He watched me keenly, as if he thought I might be hiding something.

"What? That's what it used to be. You know, for like, beef and stuff."

"I see." He rubbed his chin thoughtfully. "Are you inquiring because you have chosen to accept the facts of my presence here on Earth?"

"*Hell no*, but you tell a pretty good story."

He shrugged, acknowledging the truth of it. "I suppose the trials of the gods would make for a compelling tale among humans, yes. Had I learned of it in the way you have, I might have felt the same."

"There you go, see?" I leaned back on my hands. "And we're all the way up to the massive, world-ending battle, so you can't leave me hanging now. Tell me about this asshole in black. Does he know Rocco?"

I already knew the answer to that. Why else would he be showing up at Rocco's newest hangout? I couldn't make sense of it, though, and for the first time, I was willing to admit that maybe Marcus could clear things up.

*Maybe.*

"He is a demigod, as I have said." Marcus ran his fingers over the carved pattern in the surface of his flask. "In Carcerum, we called them Apprenti. They are, for lack of a more appropriate expression, servants of the greater gods.

Each greater god has many, and their term of service is infinite."

"Shitty gig," I remarked.

"Indeed, it would seem so. But Apprenti are powerful beings in their own right, no matter their origin. Some were human, and some were other types of creatures. Most are abominations. And all are in the thrall of their parent god. They live to carry out the greater god's ultimate purpose, whatever it may be."

"So, you're saying that guy has a boss, and I'm guessing that boss is bad news."

"The demigod we witnessed is known most often as Delano." Marcus turned the flask over in his hands. "His greater god is Lorcan."

"And Lorcan is the god of what?" I asked. "Being an enormous dick?"

"In profane human terms, yes." Marcus allowed himself a grim smirk. "He is a master of darkness and deceit. He would call himself a master of death as well, but that particular power eludes him. Still, he is not to be trifled with. If his most loyal servant is roaming the city, it can mean no good for anyone. The two of them must be stopped."

"That seems easy," I said. "God of darkness with an insanely strong right-hand man? No problem." If true, this whole setup made Rocco and his goons look like peanuts in comparison. But most of me remained unconvinced. The guy was creepy as balls, but a demigod? I just couldn't wrap my head around that.

"This is why no general rushes into battle without a plan." Marcus pushed up into a standing position, then offered me his hand. I took it. "Our first objective is to locate an old acquaintance of mine. I have much to discuss with him. But before that can commence, I need something."

"Oh, so we're a team now?" I elbowed him gently. "Nice to know it just took some good, old-fashioned dirty fighting for you to think of me as a partner."

I made light of the crippling blow to his wound, mostly to assuage the guilt I felt about it. At least his wonder drink had him ready to go again.

He headed for the door, motioning for me to follow. At the door, he stooped to scratch the cat, who had crept out of hiding. "I value your counsel, Vic. And you strike viciously. You are a good asset on the field of battle, provided you are on the correct side."

"Thanks, I think." I checked my purse and hesitated. "Do you have your sword?"

He indicated his belt. "You were too busy kicking at me to notice I had taken it back. I think that means we are even."

"I guess so."

Ever the gentleman, Marcus let me exit the apartment first.

"Where are we going?" I asked.

"Back to the water. I have left something behind."

---

THE DOCKS LOOKED ONLY SLIGHTLY MORE hospitable in the rapidly fading twilight than they had in the dead of night. We arrived there using more conventional means this time, with only mild trespassing. I made Marcus stop and wait for a few minutes, just so I could make sure the police weren't still snooping around. A patch of ground near the base of the pier was stained a dull, rusty red. I chose not to dwell on it.

"You are certain it was here?" Marcus asked. "I confess that I cannot readily remember the events of that night."

"Trust me," I said. "I can." I led him out to the end of the structure, and we stared into the gray depths of the river. "I spotted you just out there." I pointed. "Right after that meteor lit up the sky."

Marcus grinned. "I do know how to make an entrance."

I grinned back, granting him his bullshit story. We had work to do, after all.

His eyes searched the water. "How did you locate me? I assume I must have sunk rather quickly."

"The sword was glowing. I could see the shape of it like a beacon at the bottom of the river, illuminating the deep shadows. If it wasn't for that thing, I might've had to abandon you."

"I see. I am grateful." Without further ado, Marcus removed his armor and stripped off his tunic. "Wait here. I will return shortly."

"Try not to freeze down there." It made me cold just looking at him, and I was thankful that he didn't need a diving partner. One impromptu trip off the end of that pier was good enough for me.

I watched him dive into the river with surprising grace and disappear. The water seemed to swallow him whole. I hoped his wound wouldn't reactivate or somehow inca- pacitate him while he was underwater.

"Am I really worrying about this guy?" I wondered out loud. "Jeez."

Less than an hour ago, we'd been at each other's throats. Right now, we only had each other.

Marcus was gone for what felt like an inhumanly long time. I kept my gaze fixed on the choppy surface of the river, peering down for any sign of him. What the hell was he looking for, anyway? I wished I'd had the forethought to ask him. As usual, forethought was not my strong suit.

I was just getting ready to kick off my boots and dive in after him when I saw his head break the surface a few yards out from the initial site of impact. He did not appear to be carrying or dragging anything; he swam toward the dock with both arms. I was ready to help him out, but he hopped onto the dry concrete like a seal, wiping drops of water from his eyes.

"It is cold," he said.

"I tried to warn you." I picked up his tunic and held it out. He stood up, did his best to shake off the river water, and shrugged back into it. "I don't think it's cold enough for you to get hypothermia, but we should probably get somewhere warm, sooner rather than later. You were a long-ass time."

"Yes." He shook himself again. "But my hunt was miraculously successful." He reached beneath the tunic and drew up a golden chain in his fist. A medallion dangled from the shining links, engraved with a coat of arms.

"That's it?" I asked, genuinely bewildered.

"What do you mean, 'that's it?' This medallion is crucial to the next phase of our plan."

"How? You think that bling is gonna get you into a club

downtown?" I sort of laughed at my own lame joke, but, of course, Marcus didn't get it. He ignored my sass completely.

"It is evidence of my association with Kronin in the highest order. I wore it when I would carry out his missions. It is an irrefutable symbol of my authority."

"I'll take your word for it," I said. "Let's go. You're starting to soak through your tunic."

We went out the way we came, thankfully undetected. When we were safely back on normal pedestrian thoroughfares, Marcus patted his chest proudly. "This medal is a family heirloom, Vic. It is said to keep the spirits of my father and our ancestors close, should I need them." His face grew solemn. "It was of much comfort to me during the early days of my transition."

The subject felt a little heavy, so I elected not to press. "How long does it take that thing to dry?" I made a motion toward his tunic. It had soaked up most of the moisture and now hung on his frame like a sack.

He shrugged. "Its condition does not concern me. The garments of Carcerum are impervious to wear."

"Right. Then what do you say we stop in somewhere for a drink? I think we could both use one."

"I would be pleased to do so." He bundled up his armor and tucked it under his arm.

"Awesome," I said. "Just promise me, no duels with strangers, OK?"

## 18

"ANOTHER!"

A crowd was forming around us, and it sent up a cheer every time Marcus called for a new round in his trademark boisterous manner. He was a hit everywhere he went; people just drank up his friendly eccentricity. I couldn't help losing myself in the atmosphere of camaraderie he so effortlessly created. If he had been a soldier, he must have been a great one.

The bartender passed over another couple of shots. It was a familiar scenario, except I had no friend to water it down. These were full strength. But I also wasn't playing a deadly game this time, just a normal drunken one. With my weird, but lovable, friend in a damp tunic.

Marcus tipped his shot glass back, drained it in a gulp, and set it on the bar with a decisive clink. He nodded at me encouragingly. "Take your turn, Vic! I trust you are not yet bested?"

"Hardly." I took mine even faster, relishing the burn of the whisky down my throat. The crowd whistled and cheered. "Again?"

"Again." Marcus signaled to the bartender, who passed over two more shots with arched eyebrows.

"I'm not responsible if this gets out of hand," he told us. "But it's a hell of a show, and it's driving my tips up like crazy."

"Don't worry. I'm real good at holding my liquor." This much was true. Between the years of recon in grimy bars and the pathological drinking to forget my past, I'd become a regular human keg. Eight shots in, I was only starting to feel it fuzzing the edge of my mind.

For once, the sensation was pleasant instead of desperate. I was secure with someone I, at least, half trusted. And I was not on the hunt.

The shot exchange went on until Marcus tapped out at twelve, leaving me the unequivocal victor in our little match. I stood up a bit unsteadily and raised my hands above my head. The crowd, now triple the size it had been when we started hours earlier, roared.

Marcus grinned at me. His eyes were a little glazed, but he looked as happy as I'd ever seen him. "I am truly astounded, Vic," he said. "And impressed. And defeated."

"Yes! Yes, you are. You're welcome." I took the tab from the barkeep and had to look at it three times until the numbers made sense. "Hold on."

The gears ground in my head. *Shit. Do I have that much money?* I dug around in my bag for the wallet, which was now alarmingly slim. There were two fifties left in the billfold, plus another few twenties. I looked again at the bill. Just barely.

"Hey, don't worry about it, sweets." A burly guy in a leather jacket slapped some bills on the bar. "Ain't every day you get a show like that around here. I figure it's fair price for the entertainment."

"Don't call me sweets," I told him. "But thanks. I won't forget it."

He laughed. "We'll see about that."

Half an hour later, Marcus and I weaved our way out the door and down the street, aiming in the general direction of my place. He had downed half a pitcher of water and a pull from his flask. By the time we hit the stairs, he was more sober than I was.

"Are you all right?" he asked, the amusement bare in his voice. "It would be no trouble to carry you."

"Don't you dare," I growled good-naturedly. "I'm fine." He went ahead of me to the door, and I clung to the railing like a sailor to the gunwale of a pitching ship. "If I have to puke when we get inside, you can't look, okay? That's gross."

Marcus chuckled. "I promise. I am only concerned with getting you to rest. We must make an early start tomorrow."

"What?" I stopped where I was, staring up at him. "Why didn't you tell me that *before* we decided to go shot for shot?"

He held up his stupid magic flask. "Because I had a failsafe."

"That's cruel." I stumbled onto the landing, and he guided me through the door. The cat, woken from its nap atop my mattress, hurried out of the way as soon as it caught sight of me falling toward the bed.

The last thing I remembered was Marcus pulling a blanket over me. "See you at sunrise," he said. I thought he was joking.

He wasn't.

Actually, the loft was still dark when he roused me from the cocoon I had built in my sleep, nudging me with the end of a practice sword from a safe distance.

"What do you want?" I demanded. My voice was low and gravely, and it was a blessing that there was no light yet. All the shots I'd so confidently taken the night before had migrated up into my head and were knocking on my eyeballs. I groaned plaintively. "Marcus, I thought we were friends."

"We are." He nudged me again. "This is helping you. Trust me."

"I don't trust you at," I pawed for my phone and squinted into its glaring screen, "six in the morning. What time did we get back last night?"

"I do not know," he lied, smiling. "It matters not. I warned you that we must get an early start today. Your training is of the utmost importance."

"My training? Oh, *hell* no." I went to bury myself back in the blanket, but he prodded me mercilessly until I got up. "Fine. Fine! Just let me drink some water first."

A glass and a half later, I picked up my training sword and stood in front of him, eyelids still drooping. "Let's get this over with."

Marcus said it wasn't as brutal as it felt, but by the time

we actually left the loft, I was tired all over again and sore, to boot.

"You are improving nicely," he insisted, leading me down the still-darkened street.

"Yeah, yeah."

I couldn't deny that all the physical activity seemed to be helping. My sword moved with a greater purpose. It found its targets more often. Also, I noticed that I felt better about myself. Less stupid. Less like a caged animal just fighting to survive.

More like an assassin.

"Where are we going?" I called after Marcus, trotting to keep up. "And what are you doing?"

He was all over the place, checking tons of weird places for something. Under trash can lids, in dark, scary corners, in the pockets of dead-end alleyways. Every now and then, he'd stand still and gaze at the fading night sky, calculating something in his head.

He fished in a pocket of his tunic and came up with a roll of brown paper which expanded into a map. I peered over his shoulder. "Where is this? Carcerum?"

He shook his head absently. "This is your city, before it was a city."

"What? No way." I made a grab for it, but he moved the paper deftly out of my reach. "No fair. Let me see."

In response, he tilted it toward me from a distance.

It looked nothing like the New York I knew. I didn't understand most of the symbols on more than a vague level, but Marcus clearly did. He looked between the stars and his map for a moment, then turned slightly and headed in a new direction. "This way."

"How can you tell?" I asked. "That map is ancient."

Marcus smiled. "Some things never change."

His orienteering led us down a meandering path in which I failed to see the logic. We passed bars, boutique shops, garages, and subway stations. Every time I asked, Marcus wouldn't tell me what he was searching for. Finally, I made him stop on the sidewalk and talk to me.

"Dude, I know you're in the zone right now or whatever, but as long as I'm here, I might as well help. So, tell me what exactly is going on, please."

"Right." He scratched his head. "I apologize. But let us keep moving while we converse." He kept consulting the map, pausing every so often to mutter to himself. "The base of the truth is this: long ago, when gods and their ilk walked the earth, they existed among all manner of other creatures. Today, the creatures, as well as the gods themselves, are little more than memories. They have been forgotten by your world."

"Okay," I said slowly. "And what exactly are these Forgotten like? They wear armor and talk strange like you?"

"They are difficult to classify. As varied as their species were, so were their temperaments, and their crimes against the rightful inhabitants of Earth."

"That would be humans?"

"Good, you are learning." Marcus patted me on the shoulder. "So, when the time came that Kronin banned the greatest of the Forgotten to Carcerum, he gave these lesser beings a choice: to join him in Carcerum or to stay among the denizens of the Earth. A significant number of them chose to stay."

"Here? Why?" I glanced at our surroundings. They were hardly appealing.

Then again, I was biased.

Marcus thought for a minute. "There was a rift between the greater and lesser Forgotten, between those with tangible power and those who got along under the surface, making their way by staying inconspicuous. Many of these lesser found the idea of eternity alongside the gods intolerable. So, they elected to remain on Earth, bound by Kronin's rules, instead. At least then, there would be some distance."

"I mean, I guess, but it sounds like they still had to listen to him."

Marcus nodded. "Or face his wrath. And after Carcerum was founded, few dared to question the power of Kronin."

"All right." I stretched, locking my arms casually behind my head. "So that's who we're looking for, then? A lesser being?"

"Years ago, Kronin sent me to check in on a Forgotten of note who lived near this city in a swamp. Even if that swamp is long gone, he is a sedentary figure. I believe he cannot have moved more than a mile or two from his original location."

"A swamp, huh?" I smirked humorlessly. "Well, if you think we might find him in a similar environment, I have a suggestion."

"Oh?" Marcus glanced my way, curious.

"You're certain he must be around here?" I asked.

He looked down at the map again, then nodded. "Yes. I have no doubt."

I pointed down the street at a garish sign lined with dim, flickering marquee lights. The board was dingy, and the letters were faded. *GIRLS!* it read, and then, the ever reliable *XXX*.

"If you're looking for slimy, I'd start right about here."

## 19

THE BUMP and grind music was enough to revive my hang-over in almost all its former glory. I screwed up my face against the noise. "Please tell me we don't have to spend too much time in here. I think my skull might come apart."

Marcus didn't hear me over the bass. He was back in tracking mode, his gaze roving over the dark, smoky room. As my eyes began to adjust, silhouettes emerged from the shadows. They were hunched in the familiar posture of the miserable, drowning their sorrows in booze and flesh. The whole scene left a bad taste in my mouth.

I stuck close to Marcus and followed his lead, letting my eyes wander around the murky room. There was nothing of note in there, nothing I hadn't seen a million times in a million other seedy joints before. That was, except for one behemoth of a guy who sat at a corner table, leering at the world through bloodshot eyes. He was half smiling, his jowls pocked and dangling. Below the table, he seemed to become amorphous.

A shudder ran through me. "Marcus. Do you see that dude?"

"Yes." Marcus spoke low, out of the side of his mouth. "Pay him no attention. Do not let him scare you." He paused. "I believe you would tell me to 'play it cool' under similar circumstances."

"Looks like I'm not the only one learning," I said with a smile.

We wound our way closer to the stage. Out of the corner of my eye, I spotted the guy heave to his feet, rocking the whole corner table. He edged out from behind it and waddled across the room toward a door marked EMPLOYEES ONLY, which barely opened wide enough to let him through.

Marcus signaled for me to trail him, so I kept my head down and followed in his footsteps. The first thing I'd learned about recon echoed in my head. *Act like you belong.*

The employee door opened onto a long, harshly lit hallway. The walls, once white probably, were tinged a disgusting yellow with age and neglect. A rat darted along the molding—the only surprise was that there was only one.

"Do you know where he went?" I whispered. Marcus indicated a door that stood slightly open halfway down the corridor, spilling out a slice of wavering light.

Marcus went first.

He squared his shoulders, strode forward, and pushed open the door with no hesitation. We looked in on an empty dressing room, the kind with a vanity on one wall.

I noticed an odd, brownish tarp wadded on the floor. Weird. Looking closer, I picked out holes, frayed edges, suspicious bumps. I reached out and took a bit of it between my fingers, recoiling at the soft, slightly moist texture. That was about when I realized it was skin. The same skin I'd just seen adorning that creep's corpulent figure at the corner table.

"Gross!" The word leapt out before I could stifle it.

A baseball bat crashed into the side of the doorframe, splintering it. My instincts took over, by which I mean I pulled back and shrieked. The bat, wide enough to be considered more of a club, was clutched in a huge, gray-brown hand. The skin was knobby like an old log. I followed it up to see the face of the guy in the corner.

But he was different now.

There was an empty bottle of whisky sitting on the vanity, a big, heavy, square one. Marcus picked it up and flipped it over in his hand. During the next windup of the baseball bat, Marcus arced the bottle right under the guy's huge arm.

It shattered on a protruding, rock-hard jaw.

The man—was he a man? I honestly couldn't tell—reeled back, stunned. Shards of the bottle's base rained to the ground, leaving behind smudges and trickles of sludgy blood.

*Definitely not a man*, I thought, now that I could get a good look at the shape in front of us. It was more or less the right shape, but its heavy shoulders were too hunched, and its jaw was too thick and wide. The teeth were something else altogether. They jutted from the lower lip like leaning tombstones.

I had never seen anything like it. All the thoughts in my brain melted together into a stream of gibbering consciousness. Marcus' stories, I could handle. This thing that was staring me in the face, standing on two feet in the real-ass world? Not so much. There had to be a reasonable explanation—there *had* to. For the monster in front of me. The skin on the floor.

So why couldn't I think of one?

The creature raised his bat again, prompting another clean hit from Marcus with the remains of the bottle. It broke down to a nub in his grasp, his fingers dangerously close to the gleaming edges of the glass. I would've dropped it at that point, but Marcus held firm. A tooth ricocheted off the far wall, and a moment later, so did the creature's head. It left a squash-shaped dent in the plaster.

"I yield!" The voice was a wet bellow. I watched the beast clutch at his bleeding face with those gigantic mitts, attempting futilely to pick out the smaller bits of broken glass still embedded in his coarse skin. "I yield," he said again, sounding like he meant it. "I *yield*, damnit."

"Very well." Marcus made a show of setting down the neck of the bottle. He folded his arms and gazed down on his defeated opponent. "It has been a long time, hasn't it, ogre?"

Briefly, the ogre looked like he wanted to say something snide, but sense got the better of him.

"Look, Roman, I don't know what in hell's name you think you're doing here, but I can tell you, it ain't got nothing to do with me. I haven't been messing with any of that monkey business since you saw me last. Swear by it."

"Last we met, you were leading colonists to their deaths in your stinking bog," Marcus interjected.

The monstrous figure frowned. His already saggy face

sagged even more. He hadn't necessarily seemed old before, but he sure did now. I could see the rough whiskers poking out of his chin and the cataracts clouding his eyes. "I haven't run that game for a couple centuries at least. I get everything I need right here."

"And it is every bit as shameful as it should be," Marcus said. "But I am not here to inquire about such things."

A deep sigh escaped the ogre. His body deflated, expanding a few more inches around him. "Thank the King," he murmured. "I was sure Kronin sent you."

"Kronin is dead." Marcus spoke matter-of-factly, but there was a steel edge underneath the words.

The ogre paused for a second to take in the words, then laughed. Marcus's eyes hardened, and I expected the beast to die right then.

"That explains all the weird shit that's been going down around these parts lately," he croaked, dragging his knuckles over his jaw. The slack flesh rippled.

"Elaborate."

A horrid smile parted the monster's lips, revealing his janky teeth in all their uncomfortable glory. I could feel every cell in my body trying to draw away from the contents of that dressing room. He continued, taking no notice of me whatsoever. "That's the kind of thing I only give away for a price. I'm not a cheap date, you know."

He laughed again, a bumpy, hacking sound.

"The price is that I leave your overgrown forest of a mouth intact," Marcus replied. He was pretty good at this game, but the strain was starting to show on his face. His cheeks were pale and sunken. A vein stood out in his neck.

I narrowed my eyes. Was he okay?

The ogre considered the offer. "I'll give you a freebie," he snorted. "How's that? For old times' sake. The rumor mill tells me there are some Apprenti sniffing around the backside of town. Looking for recruits and the like. I guess the whole ball of yarn is finally coming undone." The smile on his lips turned cruel. "About time if you ask me."

"I did not." Marcus shifted his weight. His temples were shiny with sweat. I opened my mouth to say something, but he kept talking before I got it out. "You have not pledged your allegiance to any such recruiters, have you?"

"Ha!" The ogre gestured to his wasted form. "In this body? You gotta be kidding. I'm too old and busted to fight. Don't have the grace of Carcerum down here to keep me young. I know it, and so does everyone else. They haven't even asked." He scratched one of his chins. "Which is good, because these days, all I want is to feast and fuck. In either order."

I made a face.

"Charming," Marcus said. "Tell me, have you heard anything about a specific Apprenti? Perhaps one who prefers the color black?"

"You mean Delano." The creature nodded his heavy head. "Yeah. Haven't seen him, but I know he's around. You must know, too, don't you? Servants of Lorcan don't exactly travel under the radar too well. Ironic, isn't it?" He chuckled, and it turned into a cough.

I wanted to throw up. *C'mon Marcus. Get us out of here.* The longer we spent in the presence of this thing, the more my skin crawled. I felt like I was full of bugs.

"Is that all?" Marcus asked. He, too, looked worse by the minute.

"Look, I don't know what you're gunning for, but if you want some serious advice, don't mess with Delano. He don't screw around with any of these bleeding hearts down here. He wants killers and only killers. If they enjoy it, all the better. You get my drift?"

"I get it." Marcus moved to straighten up, but his knees buckled, and he toppled to the side.

I rushed in to support him.

"What's going on?" I demanded. "Are you okay?"

He didn't say anything, but he felt for his flask. Behind us, I heard the human gelatin cake scrabbling around. Marcus uncapped the flask. I spun around just in time to see that we were back in baseball season.

"Dammit to hell, you bastard!" I grabbed the vanity chair and hurled it with all my strength straight at the bulbous gut.

The feet of the chair dug in, and the ogre retched, but held his feet. Before he could use his bat again, Marcus regained himself.

And torpedoed the jagged piece of broken whisky bottle straight into the ogre's bulging eye.

"Shit!" I gasped.

"I planned on letting you live," Marcus said with little mercy in his voice. "But apparently your fear of Kronin's law died with him. Fortunately for the people of this city, his justice lives on."

The monster made a noise kind of like a chicken as he slid to the ground. He clutched at his face, but it was futile. The bottle cap sat flush in the eye socket, eerily almost the right size.

"We are done here," Marcus said. He took me by the

elbow and guided me from the room, back into the hall-way. We retreated from the carnage in silence. On our way out of the employee door, we passed a girl in little more than bits of pink string. Despite the fact that she could have been his daughter, she gave Marcus a flirty smile.

Neither of us said a word. The door closed. We walked away fast.

The club was loud, but we still heard her scream.

## 20

I SAVED all my words for when we were outside again in the relatively fresh air, away from that hellhole stripper prison. I started with the obvious. "Are we gonna get in trouble for that?"

"No. The body will be gone without a trace by the time the authorities arrive. The longer he has been preserved, the faster death will dissolve him."

"Okay, sure." All I could do was unconditionally accept whatever he said at this point. Denial required a presence of mind that I simply didn't have. Which led seamlessly into my next questions. "So, it's really real, then? You weren't lying?"

Marcus smiled. "I never lie. It goes against my code."

"All of it is real?"

"Yes."

I blinked. My mind remained stubborn, at least, in part. "But, like, *all* of it?"

He ran a hand through his hair and adjusted the neckline of his tunic. "Let me recount the tale of when I first discovered the truth about the realms. We were in Gaul, my cohort and I, on a regular foot patrol. This was something we did every day, several times over. For quite some time, we had seen and heard nothing. With no evidence to the contrary, we expected this trend to continue."

"Sure," I said.

"But as you can guess, it did not. We were attacked by a monster, half man and half bull, with great, wide horns and cloven hooves instead of feet. It was nearly twice my height, and it bellowed like livestock but a thousand times more terrible." An inscrutable expression crossed his face. "It is no exaggeration to say I nearly soiled my tunic on the spot."

I snorted. "No kidding. They call those things minotaurs now."

Marcus nodded. "They have always had their proper names, but it has taken me ages to learn them all. There are so many more than you know, Vic. And in the wake of Kronin's death, the curtain grows thinner every day."

"What happened after the minotaur arrived? Did you beat it?"

"No." He smiled flatly. "Our weapons barely slowed it down; it was as if its flesh was wrought from iron. I saw a man's skeleton splintered on those horns." He winced at the memory. "My men scattered, some fallen, others in shock, and others mad from the impossibility of what they were witnessing. I thought for sure that we would be destroyed, our chances at honor wiped out, but then Kronin arrived."

"He was there? You met him?" No matter how hard I

tried, I couldn't keep myself from being drawn into the captivating weave of his story.

"That is when I met him for the first time. He descended much like I did unto this plane, albeit in a vastly more controlled manner. He had the *Gladius Solis* with him then, and he used it to rend the minotaur clean in half."

"Uh huh." I knew a bit about the blade's ability to do that.

"He was so regal, so radiant, and so just and commanding that I pledged my service to him then and there. For the rest of my days, however many I had." He glanced up at the moon. "As it has turned out, I had a lot."

"And you're still serving him," I said. "Here in New York."

"I never imagined the world could look like this." Marcus took a deep breath. "Or that I would be able to see it this way." He turned to me. "This is why my mission is so important, Vic. I must protect and preserve this world because it used to be my world, too. Perhaps you do not see the same value in it as I do, but my hope is that you will someday. And I hope you will feel the same sense of duty toward your fellow human beings."

"What are you trying to say, Marcus?" I asked quietly.

He pondered that. "I am trying to say that I hope you will choose to save them when the time is right."

"That's theoretical, right? I'm trying to get rid of someone, remember?"

"Yes, but there will be many more to dispose of in the future—your future. In Kronin's absence, the darkness he kept at bay will only grow until it engulfs this world." He pointed his thumb toward the strip club. "The things you saw in that house of ill repute were only a taste of the bitter potion. There are far greater horrors biding their time in the shadows."

"Delano," I muttered.

"And more."

It was all too overwhelming. I could feel myself actually getting lightheaded. "Can you make it home okay on your own?" I asked. "Sorry, I just... I just need to take some time to think about things. About everything."

"Take your time." Marcus lifted his hand in a casual salute. "You have much to absorb. I understand."

"Thanks." I smiled tightly. "See you later, okay?"

---

I VEERED off the main streets after we parted ways. Back in the days before everything went to hell, I followed all the rules when it came to walking at night. Never alone, never unarmed. I knew how to grip my keys between my knuckles with the best of them. Now that I spent my days and nights ducking out of dangerous bars and had no problem firing a gun in crowded rooms, I'd thrown all that caution to the wind.

It was freeing in a way. In another, it was terrifying.

I turned my brain off and trusted my feet to just walk through the cool October air. The breeze lifted my hair off my neck. I ran both hands through it and let myself smile at the feeling, even though it was a little greasy. That was another thing I'd embraced about the street life: no one cared if I looked a little ragged. We all did.

We all *were*. Inside and outside.

My heart noticed that the streets were starting to look familiar, but for different reasons than I'd become accustomed to. I told myself to ignore it. The draw, however, was irresistible. In my current state of mental exhaustion, I couldn't keep myself away if I tried.

So, I didn't.

The building had been abandoned for five years, and it still stood empty, the façade bearing traces of the blaze that had taken it down. I ran my hand along the outside edge of the boarded-up front window, staring at the layer of dust that came away with my fingers. I had played in that window when I was a child. I'd practically grown up in it. My parents used to joke that half their business came in because of the baby in the front display.

Looking at it always took me back to the last day.

The cop had been young, a woman with plain blonde hair pulled up in a sensible bun. She had looked earnest, eager to do her job right. She had also looked incredibly, painfully sorry. I'd never forgotten the look in her eyes when she knelt down beside me, took my hands in hers, and told me my mother and father were dead.

That cop was nowhere to be seen a few months later. The officer who told me the investigation was effectively closed was a man, barrel chested, with the face of a garden slug. He'd been chewing tobacco while we talked. That was what I remembered about him. The tobacco.

I also remembered my unfathomable anger, and my hunger for justice to be served. So began my five-year mission to make right what the authorities couldn't—or wouldn't.

In all of it, the only kindness I tasted was from that lady

cop, with the perfect blonde bun. She was the only one who wanted to help me.

At least, until Marcus.

Now, I was beginning to feel like a person who had found motions she actually wanted to go through. I was finding things besides vengeance to care about again.

My friends. A cause bigger than me. Hell, even the stray cat Marcus would have eaten that now unequivocally called the loft its castle.

Today, like me, the front window of their shop was nothing more than a void covered by plywood, too broken and unimportant even to be revitalized. The thought made tears bite at the corners of my eyes. How could I ever believe in the concept of fairness again, after what had happened at Stratton's Checks & Cash? How could I ever see the intrinsic good that Marcus saw every time he looked out at New York?

A week ago, I would have simply said I couldn't. Now, I was beginning to sense a change stirring in the depths of my soul. I had no clue what it was, but it made me hate less. It made me wonder who I'd become and how I'd allowed myself to get here. The things Marcus had mentioned during our fight lit such a hot fire in me because they hit too close to home.

For five years, I was a living manifestation of anger, revenge, and pain. But Marcus was right. That emotion kept me a victim.

I was twenty-eight years old, almost twenty-nine, standing in front of my parents' burned-out shop and crying like a baby. I sobbed so hard that I had to kneel on the sidewalk where the drooping ribbons of crime scene tape had hung, in front of the boarded window shattered years ago.

It passed like a flash flood. I wiped at my face, thankful that whatever makeup I'd been wearing had long since disappeared. Then I stood up, took a deep breath, and smiled. Not a great smile. Certainly not my best. It was progress, though. For the first time in a small eternity, I was able to take in that store and think of happy things instead of flames and carnage.

Maybe there was more to life than vendettas after all. Maybe I *could* be a hero.

*Don't get ahead of yourself,* warned the voice in the back of my head. *Rocco Durant still deserves to die.*

True. Nothing would change that. Still, I had time, which meant I could shift my priorities a little. Marcus, on the other hand, apparently had a lot less time than me.

Shit was happening to him like crazy. I had just seen him kill a damn ogre in the back of a strip club. An *ogre.* It did not feel real, and yet, I was there. And if he was right, there was inevitably more carnage to come. There was absolutely no way to predict where this road would lead, but he'd already brought me to the first toll booth.

The least I could do was pay what I owed and continue on at his side. My personal gripes could wait—for now.

After all, we were friends, weren't we?

---

THE WALK HOME was different from the walks I'd taken over the past five years. Not different enough that I no longer saw the swarms of rats pouring in and out of dumpsters, or the loud drunk peeing on the corner of a building. There were still roaches, piles of garbage, and a million cigarette butts on the street.

None of that had changed.

But now I had a better reference point for how much things *could* suck, and they didn't suck as much as a lecherous old ogre who'd been finding various places to rot in the dark over the considerable span of his several-hundred-year life. They didn't suck as much as a Roman Centurion putting the neck of a whisky bottle in your eye.

It was screwed six ways till Sunday, but it was perspective, and that was what I'd needed for the last five years. I just didn't realize how badly until Marcus literally fell into my life.

I made a mental note to thank him in the morning. Then, as I reached the front of my building, I squinted at something out of place in the dark. The front light was out, which was weird. That thing always buzzed like it had been on continuously since 1970. And there was a silhouette lying draped across the sidewalk in front of the door.

It took one more step for me to see that it was a body.

## 21

I SHUDDERED. My stride faltered. "Oh, no."

For obvious reasons, I was not great about happening upon people who were dead, and I prayed that wouldn't be the case here. A homeless person passed out from drugs or alcohol, I could handle. Dead bodies just hit a little too close to home.

Unfortunately, it happened to be directly in front of the place where I needed to be, so I steeled myself and started forward again.

I held my breath. Part of me had dared to hope that I was mistaken about the shape. Maybe it was a discarded rug, a futon mattress, or yet more trash bags. As I approached, however, I could see that I'd been right. To my horror, I knew the person to whom the body belonged. A floppy hat was pulled down over the face.

"No, no. Sam. Please be sleeping. Please be sleeping. Please be sleeping."

I crept as close to him as I could bear, searching keenly

for signs of breathing. For half a second, I was sure he must be dead. Then, his chest rose and fell, and I almost cried with relief. I shook myself and prepared to step carefully over him.

Sam sat up. "The monsters are after you. Beware!" His hand shot out and gripped my pant leg with a terrifying strength. I clapped a hand over my mouth to hold in a scream .

"What monsters?" I asked.

He squeezed my leg. His eyes were wide and staring. The hat lay upended in his lap where it had fallen. "They're inside!" he whispered loudly. "Beware!"

He was seriously freaking my shit out. I nodded slowly. "Thank you."

He watched me edge toward the door. Never blinking.

I was glad to get into the stairwell, away from whatever was going on with him. He'd never shown signs of instability before, but maybe he'd finally run out of his last meds, or his demons had caught up with him. Adrenaline coursed through my veins. I took the stairs two at a time up every floor, not pausing until I reached my landing. My heart hammered in my chest. I produced my key, put my hand on the door handle, and it swung open.

"What the hell?" I looked down at the handle and saw that a good portion of the lock had been blown apart, probably by a gun. The breath caught in my throat. Awesome. The one night I happened to be totally defenseless was the night my place finally got broken into.

Well, I still had my fists and my feet. I pushed the door open the rest of the way with my foot, and I brought my arms up in a boxer's stance as I moved into the loft. Every muscle in my body was tense like steel cable. I must have looked confident, but I wasn't. Punches, no matter how hard, would never be an even match for a gun.

I'd been the underdog for years, but that didn't mean I had grown to like it. *Just once, I want to be the asshole with the advantage.*

"Marcus?" I moved to the light switch and flipped it.

Stars exploded across my vision. I stumbled, reflexively grabbing the side of my head before realizing I'd been hit. I turned toward the invisible source of the blow and found myself face to face with a mountain of a guy in a dark suit.

My first thought was Rocco, but it didn't take long to correct myself. The suit was too cheap. And this guy didn't have any scars.

Yet.

He pulled his lips back into an angry snarl and locked his hands around my upper arms. "You're dead meat, girlie. Worse than dead meat."

"Yeah?" I dug my feet into the floor and fought back, but his sheer bulk gave him incredible leverage. "You gonna run me through a wood chipper, or what?"

He took a step forward, and my heels slid backward along the floor.

"Don't give me any bright ideas. They'll find you in a dumpster as soon as I get what I need."

So, he was looking for something. He jerked me to the right, and the room twirled around me. All my shit was strewn across the floor. My bed was cut open, and my blankets were ripped apart. All the bottles had been smashed into a mosaic of balefully glittering broken glass, and all my crates lay in pieces. The table still stood, but even the chairs were tumbled over, to say nothing of my makeshift bathroom wall. The wreckage made it easy to see that at least the scumbags left my plumbing intact.

Where was Marcus? No way he would have gone this long without showing himself if he were present. I brought my eyes back to the guy who was doing his best to pin me against a wall. "What happened to my friend, Frankenstein?"

He furrowed his heavy brow, and his grip momentarily loosened. I used the opportunity to regain some traction in my feet and shove with all my might against him. It was like shoving into a damn brick wall. He didn't budge. He just held me still while he thought about how to answer. Was it possible he had never seen Marcus?

"Don't matter," he said after a prolonged pause. "Just tell me where *it* is."

"I don't know what you're talking about, shitbag," I answered honestly.

His lips curled back again, and with a frustrated roar, he tossed me across the room. I somehow managed to career into a piece of my ruined bed, and while I struggled to get my bearings, he let out this weird, unearthly screech. The hairs on the back of my neck stood on end.

I looked up, but there was no way to describe what I saw.

His face was morphing. The skin stretched and bubbled over a shifting skeletal structure. Teeth elongated to needle points in the growling mouth. His skin, previously blotchy and uneven, had drained of color except for the great black bags beneath his eyes. And his eyes—I almost couldn't look at them. They reminded me of the paralyzing, bloodless stare just like the man at the slaughterhouse whom I now knew to be Delano. This man, standing in my apartment, was a similar kind of creature as that demigod Marcus had warned me about.

I didn't like this one bit. I liked it even less when he came flapping at me in high gear, shoulders pushed forward, fingers curved inward like talons. If I thought my nails were in dire straits, they were nothing compared to his. I had no doubt he could slit my throat with his thumb if he wanted to.

I swallowed hard. First ogres, now vampires? Even as all this bullshit was slowly becoming real in front of my eyes, I'd had enough of it.

"All right, Twilight," I said. "Let's rumble."

The vamp was fast, but in these close, cluttered quarters, it was more of a hindrance than a help. The first time he tried to snatch me with one of his horror-movie hands, all I had to do was jump to the other side of a pile of debris. The movement was enough to throw his momentum off kilter, and he teetered precariously on his center of balance.

"I don't have time for games, foolish girl!" He had acquired a snakelike hiss in his voice—maybe because of all those fangs.

"You'd have more time if you hadn't wasted so much on jacking up all my shit!"

He scooped up a piece of a cinderblock and hurled it at my head. I felt the side of it whiz past, way too close to my face, almost grazing my cheek. It exploded into dust and shrapnel against the back wall.

"Where is it?!" he howled. His teeth glistened, and the ghostly eyes burned with a feverish hunger.

"Where's what?" I glanced at the mess on the floor. "I don't know where anything is now that most of it's in pieces on the floor. And guess whose fault that is, huh? Like an ass-ugly bull in the world's shittiest china shop."

He was not convinced or impressed. The next thing he threw was a handful of bottle pieces, which also shattered spectacularly upon impact. "Wretched imp!" he shrieked.

"Hey," I said. "Haven't heard that one before."

I crouched among my minefield of wrecked furniture since he didn't seem eager to carve a path through it himself. He was waiting for me to stray within reach of his long, sinewy arms just for a second. That was all it would take for him to end it.

We both knew that. So, we were locked in a standoff as I tried to figure out my weapon situation. I groped blindly through the debris, unwilling to take my eyes off the vampire. He was still changing, and he didn't seem to like it. His ears were longer now, and his limbs looked like they were growing, too. Creepy, sharp shoulder blades tore through the back of his shabby suit.

"Is *that* why you guys wear such cheap shit?" I asked him. He grunted, stretched out his freakishly long arms, and gathered up more things with which to pelt me. I blocked the worst of it with a chair. "It'd be real cool if you could cut that out. Like, now."

My hand hit something long on the floor, and my fingers closed automatically around a grip. I grinned. I'd forgotten about our practice swords.

Not the best, but better than nothing. I made sure my

hold on it was ironclad. The battered wooden sword was my only shot. The vamp wasn't as stupid as I wanted him to be. As soon as he caught sight of what was in my hand, he knew my game, and he flew into a frothy rage. But the full length of his limbs made him even more unwieldy in the limited space we had. I watched him knock stuff off my counter, kick the table over, and then try to nail me with the chair. A flying splinter dug into my cheek.

First blood. All bets were off.

It was reasonable to believe that the angrier he got, the more dangerous he was, but I needed him to let his guard down if I wanted to drive a dummy sword into his heart. Raw emotions were the easiest way to manipulate him without him noticing. So, I made myself stay put where he could see me. The fact that I remained alive and full of blood bothered him intensely.

He began to make poor decisions.

It started when he rose to his feet, which were now a bunch of grotesquely long, clawed toes clad in the remains of his shoes. He lurched toward me, swaying precariously on two feet with his knuckles dragging on the floor.

I wrinkled my nose as I stared into his wasted face. "Did you agree to become this? I mean, have you seen yourself? It's not pretty."

My taunting had the desired effect. His eyes blazed with fury, and he rushed at me. Once he got in range, he tried to grab me, but his swings were wild. I got the impression that he wasn't used to his body, and he didn't know how to use it effectively.

The long fingers were easy to elude; it was the nails, now fully formed claws, that made me nervous. A lucky hit could end everything, and bleeding out on my own floor was not how I wanted to die.

I adjusted my grip on the training sword. The creep was so obsessed with getting his hands on me that he'd stopped guarding himself. If I had any chance at all, it was going to come very soon. It would be even better if I could disable one of his hands for any length of time, but that was me thinking like an action hero.

*Be realistic. Focus, Vic. Just get the job done.*

Then, the grabbing arms stopped swinging. The vamp crouched on all fours, low to the floor. His eyes were trained like laser sights on me. He was going to pounce.

It was the best I could have hoped for. He might as well have gifted himself to me on a silver platter as far as I was concerned. I had the perfect maneuver in my repertoire already. All I had to do was nail the timing.

He leapt, and I swear time slowed down while his body climbed on its arc through the air. I saw each individual claw outstretched, poised to tear me to pieces the same way he'd dismantled my stuff. I saw the great, sallow plain of his upper torso, and I dashed forward to position myself underneath the right spot. As he began his descent, I swept the blade upward and thrust it with all my might into the vampire's bare hide.

The sword was dull. It took an insane effort to get that blunt, chipped wooden blade to perforate the vampire's leathery skin. A sickening, popping tear told me I'd finally achieved my goal. The weapon seemed to be sucked up into his body, at least, until the hilt bridged the wound. I'd been prepared for torrents of blood, but there wasn't much at all.

The monster's whole body stiffened. His limbs went rigid, then limp in rapid succession. I put my hands up just in time to knock him to the side as he fell, saving myself from being crushed beneath his massive form. The sword handle stuck out straight from the left side of his breast. He attempted to paw at it, but each movement of his arm got weaker and weaker.

In the last moments before life left him entirely, he started to look more human again. I averted my eyes, but I heard the thump of his limbs losing their forced tension and hitting the floor.

Silence reigned for about ten seconds. Then, a weird whispering took up, and I found out that even more of the legends were true.

The sons of bitches really did turn to ash.

---

## 22

THE FIRST THING I did after killing the vampire in my apartment was to find an unbroken glass and fill it with water, which I drank. Then, I picked up the table and its corresponding chair. I had to dig my roots into mundanity, to drag myself back into the real world. The ashes were still there on the other side of the room. Now, I saw that there were more scattered all around and mixed in with everything else.

There was also blood. But no Marcus.

The cold hand of dread squeezed my stomach. The pieces of the big picture were falling into place in my mind. Marcus had fought there and stood his ground with every ounce of honor in his body, but he must have been overwhelmed, or else he would still be around.

The loft had been tossed. The vamps were searching for something, but what? It was hard to believe there was something in my possession that they just had to have.

Then it hit me. *The sword!* Duh. I felt very, very stupid.

Of course, the vamps wanted the sword. I was willing to bet that blade put my dummy sword to shame when it came to slaughtering monsters. The only problem was this: where was the sword now? Marcus should have had it, but they wouldn't have taken him with them if they found everything they wanted. And they wouldn't have left old dry bones around for me.

They still hadn't found what they needed. Hopefully, that meant Marcus was still alive.

A tiny mewing came from the cracked window. When I saw the cat clinging to the outside sill, I rushed over and scooped it up into my arms, momentarily overcome with a rush of concern for something other than myself or Marcus. "Sorry, baby." I stroked its soft ears. "Glad you're okay."

I spent a few minutes pacing restlessly around the loft, holding the kitten and clearing a path in the rubble of my life as I tried to figure out my next steps. Obviously, I needed to go after Marcus. There was no way I was leaving him at the mercy of a pack of vampires. That being said, I was not foolhardy enough to attempt a rescue on my own.

Fishing Marcus out of the river was one thing. A potential vampire den was a whole other ballgame. I was going to need reinforcements, and my options were limited. There was really only one person I could even consider asking for help.

Except, I didn't want to consider Deacon St. Clare. I would've been perfectly happy to never see him again. Too bad I didn't have a choice. I stopped pacing, put down the cat, retrieved my phone from my bag, and frowned. I also did not have his contact information. Then, I remembered how I'd met him the first time, and my eyes lit up.

*Bingo.*

Jules answered on the second ring. "Hey, Vic. What's up?"

"Sorry I'm calling at such an odd hour," I said. "I was wondering if you could do me a favor."

"You know the answer to that without having to ask," she said. "Name it, and it's yours."

"Okay." I bit my lip. "Do you have Deacon's number?"

Jules giggled. The giggle escalated into more of a cackle. "I knew it!" she crowed triumphantly. "You totally like him."

"I mean—"

"It's okay, Vic. Just admit it! Like anyone would blame you. We all saw him." She paused. "Not sure if he'd be down for the late-night booty call, though. I don't know what kind of guy he is."

I felt myself blushing, more out of annoyance than embarrassment. "*This* is not a booty call! He… wanted me to follow up with him after the whole thing at East Coast Comics Convention. And I lost his number. So, I need it from you. That's all."

"Well, I don't know it either," Jules said, with genuine regret. "But I do have Ezra's, and Ezra is the one who invited him."

I pinched the bridge of my nose, painfully conscious that valuable time was passing. "I just need to get in touch with him. No booty calls for anyone."

"Okay, okay." Her tone of voice told me she didn't

believe a word I said. "I'll call Ezra as soon as we hang up, and then I'll text you. Good luck!"

"I don't need luck," I protested, but she was gone already. A couple minutes later, my phone buzzed with Deacon's number.

I took a deep breath and called it.

---

"St. Clare."

Even over the phone, his voice did weird things to me. I forced myself to focus on the problem at hand. I had to find a way to convince him to believe me, and then, to agree to help me.

*Here goes nothing.* "Hi. It's Vic."

"Vic?" He hesitated, either recalling me or trying to decide whether or not he should hang up. "Ah, right. Sexy woman in high heels who likes to hang out with gangsters."

I rolled my eyes. "That's me. Listen, I need your help."

"What kind of help?" That was when I discovered that Deacon and Marcus shared the ability to flick that suspicious undertone on and off at a moment's notice.

"Jules gave me your number," I said quickly. "She got it from Ezra. And she thinks I'm using it for... other things." *Why did I just say that?* I forged on, privately mortified. "Anyway, it's about Durant."

"I'm listening."

I considered telling him the whole story—for half a second. But Deacon seemed like a reasonable person, which meant I would sound crazier than Marcus. I decided that in this case, slightly altering the truth was an acceptable moral compromise.

"You remember my friend, Marcus, from the party?"

"Who could forget that tunic?"

"Well I'm pretty sure that Durant and his goons have kidnapped him. I came back to my apartment and there was blood everywhere and Marcus he... Rocco would want him bad. They're going to kill him unless we stop them."

The line hung silent for a second before Deacon responded. "How do you know all this?"

*Dammit.*

"Listen," I said. "We don't have time to play twenty questions here. You know I'm...connected somehow. And I know I was kind of a dick back in the prison, but you're just going to have to trust me on this. Please. If not, Marcus will die."

"Okay. Okay," he said. "But we do it my way. Durant lives to see his day in court."

"Fine, whatever," I said. And I meant it. Marcus's life meant far more than my revenge.

"Tell me where they're at. I'll call in the local PD, and we'll sort this whole thing out. You have nothing to worry about."

But that wasn't true, and as soon as he said it, I knew this planned was doomed to fail. The local cops, there's no way they'd be prepared for this. If what I just faced in my apartment was anything like what was waiting at the factory, then Deacon and his men would be torn to shreds. I didn't even know if their guns would work on vampires or demigods or whatever else kind of hell Durant had locked away.

But I knew something that would.

"Vic?"

"I'm sorry, Deacon." I searched for the words to say, but nothing came. So I mumbled, "I'm sorry," once again and hung up the phone.

I was alone again, but this time I had a plan. If Marcus had hidden the sword, and it wasn't in the loft, then there were good odds I knew where it would be.

The only other place he knew.

I didn't bother locking the door behind me—I just ran full tilt down the stairs and out of the building. Sam was gone, but I didn't have time to worry about him. The docks weren't that far, but I was terrified that every wasted second could cost Marcus his life.

My priorities had a lot to learn. Or maybe I did, since they belonged to me. Find a way to rig a proper shower in the loft? Eh. Focus on making myself some real food once in a while? Whatever. Go diving for a magic sword in the river on a mid-October night? Yes.

In my defense, it wasn't like I had a choice. I had to find the sword. I *had* to. Marcus's life depended on it, and I was increasingly afraid that mine now depended on his. Plus, it was a point of pride. I couldn't save a guy, sort of befriend him, and then let him get kidnapped and murdered on my watch. Totally unacceptable.

So yeah, I needed that sword badly.

Then, I needed to use it to wreak havoc on my enemies.

All right. So maybe that last part didn't sound so bad.

## 23

THE RIVER LOOKED black beneath a cloudy sky, and faint moonlight glinted off the surface current. It reminded me a lot of the night when it had all started. Not so many days ago, actually. Hardly any.

I barreled down the runway of the stone pier, my eyes fixed hard on the point in space where I thought Marcus had initially gone down. I didn't even pause before I leapt out over the river.

The water came up around me like a thousand tiny needles. Once again, I gasped, pushed down my natural inclination to head for dry land, and dove deeper toward the bottom. The first thought that occurred to me was: *I have never seen a black as black as this.* Not only was there no light, but it seemed like light could not survive beneath the water. My eyes being open made almost no difference.

After twenty seconds of slow diving and searching, I returned to the surface, took in a gigantic gulp of air, and submerged again. My face and hands were rapidly numbing, and my eyeballs felt like spheres of ice, but I pushed through it. Leaving the sword behind was one hundred percent out of the question. What if it was the only thing that could kill Delano's monsters?

The current kept pulling me away from the area I wanted to be in. I had to surface twice more before I managed to get down far enough for it to matter. I opened my eyes as wide as I could and peered through the inky murk at nothing. My hair drifted around my face like kelp. It was probably going to freeze solid when I got out.

*If* I got out. Because I was only getting out after I located the sword. I kicked harder, cutting the water apart with my hands. The air in my lungs was running low. At the edge of needing to turn back, I caught a glimpse of something down at the very bottom. A glowing shape.

The sword!

I replenished my air supply and dove with renewed vigor, shooting downward in a rush of bubbles. My clothes dragged at me, but the sheer determination overrode all of that. As I got nearer, the glow seemed to intensify, almost as if the hilt was calling me. It was stuck diagonally in the muddy bed, and when I was close enough to grab it, the water was lit so brightly it was almost clear.

I stretched out my hand, grasping the hilt firmly against my palm. It stuck for a moment, and a flash of fear leapt through my chest. I couldn't get it out. It was trapped there. It would be lost forever because of my weakness.

*Screw that,* I thought and redoubled my efforts.

Satisfaction filled my body as the hilt loosed itself from the river's clutches and came with me to the surface. I held it to my body, swimming with one arm back to the pier.

The hilt came to rest on the concrete with an unceremonious clatter, and I pulled myself out beside it. Taking the moment to look at the ancient artifact, I breathed a sigh of relief. Marcus was smart; he had the wherewithal to hide Kronin's weapon before he got nabbed by the goon squad.

I paused to wring out my hair and clothes as best I could. Against the ground, the sword hilt still glowed faintly. If I rested my bare palm on the dock, I could feel something radiating outward from it.

Energy? Heat?

Power.

I picked it up and hefted it in my palm. The moment I touched it, its light intensified. Nice of the gods to design a multipurpose device. It was warm, too, which was a welcome relief on my icy hands. As a tentative experiment, I swung it in a gentle arc until it was poised above my head.

A flash and a crackle ran through me, and suddenly, the sword was whole. Up close, it looked like it was made of solid fire. I could smell it burning. The wash of heat that had emanated from the resurgence of the blade dried me immediately.

It made me feel, somehow, as if I was taller, more capable. Able to take on the world.

"Whoa," I whispered. Maybe I could get used to this. Still, I lowered the hilt until the blade went away, and then I stashed the sword in my bag. Now that I knew it worked, I had to keep it on the down low. I couldn't have a sword out yet; not where I was going.

I doubted the bus driver would take kindly to that.

THIS LATE AT NIGHT, the buses arrived sporadically in this part of town. I was impatient at the stop and impatient in my seat, keenly aware of the sword's hidden weight on my lap and also irrationally afraid that I'd somehow set off the blade, punch a hole into the side of the bus, and possibly skewer an innocent passerby. It was safe to say the ride was tense. I couldn't wait to be out in the open again.

More specifically, I couldn't wait to fight. There was something about the God King's sword that felt so cathartic to me. Maybe it was just the fact that I'd used it for straight-up murder right from the outset, or that it cut through flesh and bone as easily as if they were butter. I wanted to use it again, and I knew the slaughterhouse—an apt venue for this confrontation—would provide me with ample opportunity.

My stop came up. I pulled the cord and hopped down the steps, like any other twenty-something without a car in New York City, which was most of them. No one knew I hadn't had honest money in years or that I scrounged for everything. And no one knew I was going to commit several acts of murder in less than five minutes.

That was my real secret. For the moment, I kept it without guilt. After all, my body count was already up to four, counting the vamp in the loft. Although, I was a little unclear on the ethics of killing monsters. No one knew better than me how little the inhabitants of the slaughter-house deserved to live. The humans alone had taken every-thing from me, and now they had seemingly made some sort of deal with the devil. If I didn't stop them in their tracks, they would take and take and take.

It was time to settle a long-uneven score.

I didn't mess with the doors at all on my second infiltration attempt. No time or patience for that. Instead, I went straight for a first-floor window that was missing its pane, shimmying delicately through the gap. The inside of the building was cloaked in shadows. It smelled like bleach. Each footstep sent a ripple of nerve-wracking echoes ricocheting off the bare walls. Sneaking was more or less impossible.

That was fine. I wasn't feeling very stealthy anyway.

I did want to explore a little bit, though. I tiptoed down the long, wide main chamber. The ceilings were high, with vents and fans. In some places, the inside wall had begun to crumble. It matched the floor which was patchy at best. Some of the biggest cracks ran the width of the entire floor. I was constantly crunching on pebbles and other debris.

"Shh!" The sound cut through my own personal noise. I stopped dead, head tilted to listen. "Someone's coming!" It was an undoubtedly female voice, high-strung and shrill with agitation.

As I resumed walking, the sound of crying filtered down to me from above. I realized there was more than one woman. The implications filled me with equal parts unease and fury. What were they doing here? Why were they crying?

I had the feeling I didn't want to know, but I was going to find out.

"Down there. Look!"

When I wasn't on the move, the slaughterhouse was so silent that any speech at all sliced through the air like a knife. Aside from some difficulties caused by the echo, I had little trouble homing in on where the voices were coming from. The moment I laid eyes on their situation, a grimace spread across my face.

They were in a cage. It was like a huge birdcage with a domed top and padlocks on the doors, swinging from an anchor chain as wide around as my waist. Several sets of frightened eyes peered out at me from the interior. They whispered among themselves.

"Who is that?"

"She doesn't look like one of them."

"I've never seen her before."

I stepped closer, and they all immediately fell silent. "Hey," I called. "I'm not a bad guy. I can get you out."

The women inched closer to the bars of the cage, eyeing me curiously. The one in front had bright blue eyes and a flowing mane of deep red hair. She gestured to the contraption enclosing them. "Out of this?" she asked skeptically. "Without killing us, I hope."

I smiled slightly. "No killing. Not of you guys, anyway." I withdrew the hilt from my bag.

Big Red frowned. "What's that? A pry bar?" She shook her impressive head of hair. "That's not gonna work."

"Better than a pry bar." I lifted it high and willed the blade to appear. The women gasped. Big Red's eyes went wide with shock and fascination. I nodded at her. "I'd stand back a little if I were you."

She seemed transfixed by the blade. They all did.

I judged the distance carefully, brought it up over my head, and then down in a slicing arc. The cutting tip of the sword struck through the padlocks, sending them clattering to the floor. The iron door swung open on screeching hinges.

"They definitely heard that," I said. "Climb down fast, and get out fast. You can use the windows. They don't all have glass."

Their feet hit the ground, and the captives fanned out to choose their escape routes. I saw that they were all around my age or younger, all slender, all pretty. All stolen for the benefit of the monsters who lurked elsewhere in the building, converging on the point where I stood sentry.

"Go," I said, waving the women on. "You can't be here when Rocco shows up. I don't doubt for one damn second that he'll kill you."

Big Red was the last to flee. She paused with one foot on the windowsill and looked back at me. "Who are you?" she asked.

I stared back at her. "I'm the woman who is about to start a war against the gods."

The beat of approaching footsteps only supported my command. Her eyes lingered on my face for a split second longer before she disappeared into the night. I let myself relax a bit. With the prisoners gone, it would be just me and Rocco, plus however many hapless goons he brought to the fight.

That much, I could handle. It would be just like before.

Except this time, Rocco Durant was not going to escape.

## 24

HE AND HIS men came up from behind me, but the persistent echo in the massive room gave me more than enough warning. The blade had once again evaporated back into the hilt, but I had the motions down now. I was ready to whip it out at a moment's notice.

Rocco looked like a million bucks, for reasons I now marginally understood. His time machine had taken him back another five or ten years, but I noticed it couldn't do shit about that nasty scar. No matter how strong his build, or how sleek and dark his hair, he'd be marred forever by that mark.

And that meant he could never hide.

He only had two dumb flunkies in tow this time. I thought about warning him that this really wasn't going to be a fair fight, but he had never cared when the odds were tilted in his favor. Why should I care if they were tilted in mine?

I wasn't here to bet. I was just here to make sure this

scumsucking shitbucket didn't make it out of here on his own two legs. He looked me up and down from ten feet away. A wicked sneer curled his lip.

"Take care of her, boys," Rocco said. "Just make sure you leave some for me."

I stifled the urge to gag. This man might not have looked like the ogre lurking in the seedy strip joint, but he was at least as repulsive, if not more. In Rocco's case, there were no excuses, flimsy or otherwise, about his base monster instincts. Rocco hadn't been abandoned by the gods, and he hadn't been stuck in his ways for centuries.

No, he was just a mean, selfish little prick whose utter delight in torture and pain were likely just his way of over-compensating for deficiencies south of the border. I'd seen it all before: flashy car, fat stacks of cash, jewels bigger than his teeth, and yet, no way to truly satisfy anyone.

This line of thought made me smile in spite of myself. It was hard to be afraid of him when I knew I had a seemingly indestructible sword of light in my hands. Marcus had mentioned offhandedly that the garments of Carcerum were more or less immune to serious damage, hadn't he? Well, if his tunic could withstand anything, I bet Kronin's trusty sword could, too. I was on the verge of getting a chance to prove it.

Rocco's goons closed in on me from either side, and I belatedly recognized them as the bro-dudes guarding the door on my first failed foray into the slaughterhouse. If they knew who I was, their chiseled stone faces betrayed nothing. They wore their sunglasses inside, where the lighting was already suboptimal.

It was almost too easy.

I made a show of stretching out the arm that held the hilt of the sword, as though I was casually prepping for a fight. The shining blade popped into existence. I caught all three of the bastards' expressions as the sword's light momentarily engulfed them. Surprise. Annoyance.

For Rocco, was there fear? If it wasn't there yet, it would be real soon.

Or else I hadn't done my job.

The beefy guards stuttered in their advance. The sword made them nervous, and that pleased me greatly. Despite the impassive reflection of their sunglass lenses, I knew they were hesitating, having second thoughts. Maybe for the very first instance in their miserable lives, they were regretting their choice of career.

"Oh, don't be afraid of that rat!" Rocco barked. His voice was harsh, a far cry from the smooth, manipulative tones I'd heard from him during our jaunt to the docks. His face was shellacked in a thin sheen of sweat, and although he continued to talk a mean game, he didn't move an inch. "She ought to have drowned in the river days ago. Clean her up!"

"Come on, boys." I smirked. My tongue ran across my lips. "You heard the boss. It's time to do his dirty work."

They didn't appreciate my taunting. The hulk on the left knitted his brows. He took something out of his pocket. The gesture gave me flashbacks to Pencil-Boy and his silver gun, but this one had a wide, flat barrel, square and painted neon yellow. I couldn't shake the feeling that I had seen something like it just recently.

My memory suddenly kicked in. This dick had a taser.

Probably because he didn't want to kill me. He had been instructed to torture me first.

Getting tortured was most definitely *not* on my agenda.

"Shoot!" Rocco commanded from the background peanut gallery. "What the hell is wrong with all of you today? I swear, it's like all your cocked-up brains are on the same shitty wavelength."

The man sure had a way with words. I tuned him out as my focus homed in on the guard's trigger finger. Of course, it was possible that they both had tasers, in which case, I'd get hit full force as soon as I lopped off the first guy's hand.

That meant I'd have to take care of them both in one fell swoop, just to be safe. You know, no big deal.

Actually, since I had this radical sword, it really wasn't that big a deal. I didn't even have to draw back that far to start my swing, and the blade still connected before he had time to do anything with that sad little taser. His hand flew away in a blur. The other guard stopped to watch it catapult off into another part of the room. All three of us heard it land with a distant thud.

The taser went off, and I laughed.

"Little late on that," I said.

His mouth dropped open at the delayed revelation that he was now in need of a prosthetic. But instead of blood, rough dust poured from the stump, coating the sleeve of his black suit and dotting the surface of his shirt. He grabbed his wrist with his good hand, but there was no stemming the tide.

Was this just a clubhouse for vampires?

I chopped off his other hand. I didn't even have both of

mine on the sword. It felt about the same as cutting a pat of butter for pancakes. No effort. No fuss.

A lot more screaming, though. The dude had finally found his voice, and he was using it to full effect. I caught a few choice words in there, but it was mostly unintelligible. His life force was draining from two grievous amputation wounds now, and since I'd carelessly cut off more of his left arm than his right, his balance was off as he wheeled to face his beloved boss.

Rocco didn't look away from the spectacle, but his face was pale as a sheet. He pressed his lips together until they almost disappeared. The guard fell to his knees. "Boss," he whispered. "B-Boss..." He teetered and fell back into the spreading pool of dust. It billowed up around the outline of his body.

Somehow, through all of that, he was still wearing his sunglasses.

I expected him to turn to ash, but he didn't, not quite. His body stiffened, turned white, and crumbled into bits of stone.

*Well, would you look at that.* What the hell was going on in this place? Not that I cared if the bastards died different, as long as they all died.

"Next," I said. My poker face remained completely undisturbed. The feeling of horror I had gotten from murdering Pencil Boy and his two unfortunate colleagues was far away, a barely recognizable sliver of human emotion. I was a human heart encased in a machine. Maybe this would all matter to me later. Maybe I'd be horrified by what I had just done and what I was about to do.

But right then, I felt nothing except the vague satisfaction of checking items off a list. One goon down, one to go. And then, the literal boss battle.

Assuming he didn't duck out on me first. Rocco still hadn't budged, but it was clear he'd been thinking about it ever since his guy lost a hand in less than the blink of an eye. He looked over at the remaining bro-guard. I did, too.

Bro-guard stood more or less frozen where he'd stopped when the sword came out, jaw slack, his reflective gaze directed toward his mangled buddy.

"I'm sorry you had to see that," I told him. He turned to me as if he didn't speak the language. "And that you had to become collateral damage. I'd let you live, but that wouldn't really be fair to your friend, would it?"

The dude's mouth moved, but nothing came out. He adjusted his sunglasses with the side of a shaking finger. If my emotions hadn't all been sucked into the tide of hatred that overtook me every time I was anywhere near Rocco Durant, I might have felt bad. Then again, he was probably just going to burst into flames the second his body hit the floor. Or turn into an ice sculpture, or some crazy shit.

These people were not people. At this point, I was ready to bet my life that neither was Rocco Durant.

Finally, some sound came out of bro-guard's craw. "I'll see you in hell, bitch!" he shouted.

Hardly original, but I couldn't blame him. He'd been through a lot in the past few minutes. Lucky for him, it would all be over soon. I gave ground as he charged me, but only so I could better line up my shot. There was a minor snafu; I had misjudged either his distance or his speed, so his massive shoulder struck me in the upper chest.

All of the breath pushed out of my lungs. I could already feel the area bruising, but that wasn't enough to stop the indomitable blade of my magical sword from penetrating clean through the center of his chest cavity. He choked and grasped wildly at the protruding end of the sword. The parts of his hands that touched the shining blade were vaporized into nothing, not even ash.

He started to slide toward me. A flurry of panic kicked up in my chest. This guy was probably at least two hundred and fifty pounds, on the conservative side. I'd be totally screwed if he managed to pin me under his dead weight. Securing my other hand on the sword hilt, I drew on all my powers of adrenaline and thrust forward with a mighty yell.

Instead of simply levering him off me like I'd intended, the extra force split the guard almost in two. As I'd predicted, he dried up and crumbled the way his cohort had done. I'd be lying if I said it didn't lessen the impact somewhat. It made it easier to kill them knowing they were real-deal monsters.

I did not look at the horrible mess the two-part fight had made. There was no blood or gore on me or the sword. I guessed it was part of the god magic or something—or the fact that no one but me seemed to have blood at all. But I had single-handedly managed to return the old slaughter-house to its roots.

I wasn't through yet. My eyes locked onto Rocco Durant. "Your turn."

He pretended to ignore me. He had long since averted

his eyes from the ultimate fate of his bodyguards, and as I moved up on him, he lit a fancy cigarette with a gold lighter. "I suppose we can't talk about this, can we? Make some kind of deal?" He chuckled, his throat dry. "Nah, who am I kiddin'?" He made a motion with the burning cig toward the remains of his goons. "You weren't into that last time, and something tells me you're not gonna be into it now."

"Nope." I summoned my trusty blade. "And I came equipped to get even more up close and personal. Aren't you glad your boys left some for you?"

I got no answer, but he didn't look glad. He looked like the coward I'd known him to be since the day he brought his gun into a check cashing shop and emptied it into my parents. I'd known he was a coward since he went back to burn down the store, so scared of getting caught that he was more than happy to pile crime on top of crime.

I hoped he was scared to die.

"This is gonna come back and bite you someday, doll-face," he said. "You know that, don't you? Little bitches like you don't just get to come in and mess with the big dogs any way you like. Even if you bring whatever the hell that thing is to the table." The sword cast his face in an orange-red glow. I brought it closer. His façade of bravado crumbled a little more.

"You always struck me as more of a cat person anyway, Rocco," I said conversationally. "On account of the way you kept slipping through my fingers before. But it looks like your nine miserable lives have finally run out."

The edge of the blade hovered inches from his bare skin. Its ambient heat burned his throat. Rocco winced.

"Wait." The word was more like a croak as it left him. The veins in his neck and forehead stood out. "Wait a damn second."

"Give me a real good reason," I told him.

"Sure." He licked his lips. "You kill me, and your friend in the getup dies."

What the hell did he mean by 'the getup?' I frowned in consternation, and then I recalled whose sword I was holding in the first place.

Vic Stratton, Friend of the Year.

"Where is he?" I asked.

Rocco grinned, the definition of shit-eating if ever I saw it. "I knew that would get your attention," he said. "Gotta say, toots, you don't look like the type who'd be into older men."

"I wouldn't push your luck." I jabbed the sword at him again so that he flinched. "Show me. If I find out you're lying, you don't get a second chance."

I backed off just enough to give him room to move. Rocco straightened his shirt and jacket and adjusted his gaudy tie. "You know, you mighta done real well in the mob," he mused. "You know how to drive a hard bargain. And you're a stone-cold bitch."

Now that he had some leverage, his cool was back in place. I wanted very badly to remind him of the man he'd been only minutes ago, who had watched his two under-lings die without lifting a finger to help.

Instead, I exercised a mammoth amount of restraint and let him lead me toward a door that opened on a stair-well. "Your buddy's up on the factory floor," Rocco said. "At the top. I think they brought him up there so that if he kept giving them trouble, they could just toss him off and be done with it." He chuckled at his own joke.

I said nothing. Why was he talking to me like we were business associates and not mortal enemies? The effect was a little disquieting. Did he think he could finagle a way to turn me to his side? Because I would rather have swallowed the sun.

We emerged onto the second floor, which was even more open than the first. Hunks of broken machinery littered the walls and floor, among them a few pieces that looked like they might still work. Vicious meat hooks hung from a section of the ceiling.

I was looking at them when Rocco Durant turned to me and asked, "Why can't you just let this go?"

"ARE YOU SERIOUS?" I glared at him, rethinking the choices I had made which allowed him to live long enough to ask me a question like that. "You *fucking* murdered my parents, and you want to know why I can't just let it go?"

If I'd expected him to be contrite, I was in for some disappointment. Rocco shrugged, raising his eyebrows.

"Your parents had it coming. Dad was weak. Running a damn check-cashing joint and he didn't even have the balls to skim a little off the top. Complete fucking waste. He went down without a fight. But your mom…"

I clenched my teeth. "What about my mom?"

His laugh was pitying, which pissed me off even more. "Your mom was a real fighter. Who do you think gave me this scar?" He pointed to the red line running down his face. "She was like you, just couldn't let things go. Doing her in was a real pleasure, believe me."

My blood was boiling, but I resisted the urge to run

him through right here. Marcus was waiting. I brandished my sword at his back. "Keep walking, Durant."

He obliged but did not shut up. "Don't get me wrong on this. I love women. You're all beautiful, angelic little slices of heaven. But you've got the jaws of a pit bull. You need to learn to let things go. Know what I'm saying? Release that negative energy."

To illustrate his point, he made a fluttering, releasing motion with his hands while I looked on in total disbelief. Who in the seven hells *was* this guy? I'd spent so much time building him up as my nemesis, imagining the final show-down in loving gruesome detail. Then, I got here after years of unimaginable pain, and he just told me I needed to release my negative energy? This felt even more surreal than all the god stuff, times a million.

"Hey, I got a question for you," I said, mostly to direct the stream of his incessant word vomit somewhere other than the topic of my parents. I didn't think I could stomach hearing any more of his bullshit without killing him, and I really wanted to get Marcus back. It seemed easier than trying to get him to shut his trap entirely.

"Shoot," he said.

"Funny you should mention that. Remember the bullet wound I gave you in the leg as you were running away like a huge asshole?" He acknowledged it with a grunt. "What happened to that? You're not limping even a little bit. You seem fine. There aren't any bandages or blood. What gives?"

He grinned. "Good question, and since you're already on a backstage tour, I'll show you our little secret." The grin widened. "In fact, I'm pretty sure that's where they took your friend."

My stomach dropped. It wasn't what I wanted to hear. "Pick up the pace," I said. "No more stalling."

Rocco held up his hands. "Relax." He pointed to a pair of heavy double doors set into a thick wall. "We're almost there."

"Good." I hoped that my clenched jaw did enough to disguise my apprehension. Whatever I was going to find behind those doors, I already knew it was going to be bad.

I just didn't know how bad.

An incongruously high-tech pad was mounted to the wall. Rocco laid his hand on it. It beeped, and an industrial lock disengaged. "Get ready," Durant said. "The show's about to start."

He turned the handles and pushed with both hands, letting the doors swing open through the force of their own considerable mass.

An intolerable noise assaulted all my senses. I clamped my hands over my ears to try and stifle the unearthly wailing, but it was no use. "What the shit is that sound?" I yelled at Rocco. He did not seem disturbed in the slightest.

On the contrary, he was obscenely delighted.

"It's the sound of *progress*!" he shouted back. "Don't stop now, sweetheart. You're already in over your head!"

With that, he continued into the next chamber, and having no alternative, I followed him. I guessed very quickly that the walls in this section must have been soundproofed. Maybe that was why the rest of the place still looked like a dump. But why did they need that? And *seriously*, what was that sound?

In the next two seconds, I found out and immediately wished I hadn't.

Rocco led me farther into the room, and I realized we were standing on a platform above a recessed pit, which was the source of the earsplitting cacophony. Why? Because it was stuffed full of screaming, writhing people.

"What…" I lost the words mid-sentence and had to stop to find them again. "What the literal *fuck* is this?"

"Welcome to America's first vampire factory," Rocco Durant said.

The words took a long, long time to register in my brain, but that might have been due to the fact that time had apparently slowed down since I laid eyes on the pit. I simply couldn't comprehend it on a basic level. The people down inside it twisted in ways I didn't think a human body was physically able to contort, and they seemed to be lashing out at each other with wild abandon.

"What are you doing to them?" I whispered the question. Rocco heard me anyway. He leaned in close.

"Nothing they didn't ask for. Well, maybe they didn't know exactly what their reward would be, but every person in that pit wanted something. To serve a higher power. To escape from their miserable lives. To gain power. It's a service we now provide. Those lucky scrubs down there are in the process of becoming Grade-A, top of the food chain, bloodsuckers. You know what I'm talking about, right?"

"Yeah," I said absently. "But how? How could you do this?"

"You wanna talk mechanics?" Rocco raised a brow, plainly impressed. "All right, we can do that." He raised a hand to signal one of the workers around the pit. "Hey, Louie! Cover that shit up, would you?"

Louie yanked a lever. I stared, dumbstruck, as a retractable lid began to roll out over the mass of bodies, plunging them into darkness. When it was fully extended, the cover dropped the noise level significantly, but it still left me feeling sick.

"You just... leave them in the dark like that? To fight each other?"

"Light levels don't matter," Rocco said dismissively. "Improved vision in all conditions is one of the first effects to manifest. They can see just fine. And I wouldn't call it fighting," he added. "This batch is brand new. They got a few days to go before the final result. So, they don't know shit about who they are or what they're doing in there. We don't even know if they can feel pain at this stage. So..." Again, he shrugged. "It's not an issue of humanity. They ain't human anymore."

I blinked, urging my brain to process the unthinkable thing I'd just heard. This was so far beyond anything Rocco had ever done to me or anyone else—and he was doing it to dozens of people at a time.

"You give them something?" I asked. "To start it?" My language capabilities were failing me on a grand scale. I could only form short, easy sentences.

It made me think of the way I'd been in the days immediately following my parents' murders. But instead of the crushing, soul-rending pain, I was just numb. Unbelieving. Despite it happening literally right in front of me.

"It's blood," Rocco said. "Don't ask me whose. I don't know. As far as this shit is concerned, I'm low on the totem pole—forgive my political incorrectness." He passed me a dickish smile before continuing. "I don't get told too much. I just get the cases from the big guy, who gets 'em from the bigger guy."

"Who's the big guy?" I hazarded a guess. "Delano?"

"Figured your friend mighta told you about him." Rocco reached into his inside pocket and withdrew a capped syringe containing an unmistakable red liquid. "Yeah. So, he brings it to us, and we put it into these things. Then..." He mimed a jabbing motion into the side of his neck. "Needle straight into the carotid, you know? Starts working inside of thirty seconds. We toss 'em in the pit because the initial injection drives them crazy. Gotta be careful though, give them too much, and it really fucks them up. Takes a few days for them to come back to their senses." He paused. "Delano said it took me two." He said this with a hint of pride, as if it was proof of his higher breeding or superior intelligence.

"You're a vampire?!" Honestly, I had no idea why I felt even an iota of surprise. I'd suspected it anyway, hadn't I? So many triple curve balls had already been thrown my way that I should have been prepared for one more.

"You asked about the deal with the gunshots," he answered. "That's it. I heal like *that* these days." He snapped his fingers. "Useful. You should try it."

"Yeah, no thanks." I directed my gaze back toward the pit and the furious melee that I knew was churning under that cover. "What happens to them after that?"

I was horrified but also fascinated. This was so far beyond the already expanded limits of my imagination. If

Marcus had told me about it from the start, I might have been way more on board with hunting this guy down.

Or I would have left him on the street. That was more likely.

"If they survive the party, then they'll be more or less back to their normal selves," Rocco said. "They can get all of that insane shit under control mostly. But they're stronger than they'd ever dreamed of being, and they're big-time hungry. They wanna eat all the time, you know? Kinda like having kids, but these ones eat other people." He leered at me. "They like young girls the best. Around your age."

I made sure he could feel the warmth of the blade at his back. "So, the cage on the first floor?"

Rocco nodded. "That was supposed to be our food supply for the next while." He signaled for the pit to be uncovered, and every muscle in my body tensed. I prepared to run him through if he tried anything untoward.

"Don't even think about it," I warned. "You'll be dead before you hit the ground."

"No, no," he said quickly. "Not you. I just said that because I like to see that look on your face. No, we've got someone else lined up. He's all ready to go." Another hand signal. Louie opened a gate in the wall and extracted a hunched over form bound in chains. I recognized the sturdy build and the tunic that was still draped over his torso.

My stomach knotted. "Don't you dare."

Louie dragged Marcus to the edge of the pit and looked up, waiting for Rocco to tell him it was time. I wanted to run over there and kill Louie, but I knew it was a fool's errand. As soon as the pressure of the sword was off him, Rocco would find a way to screw me over. He'd always been maddeningly good at that.

And then we'd both be dead.

Marcus glanced at me and shook his head. I knew what it meant. He was telling me to leave him. To let him go. To walk away.

Like hell.

"I see you understand the situation." Rocco preened, pleased with himself. "I'd apologize for making you watch, but the truth is, I'm not sorry." Busting up into waves of hearty guffaws, Rocco motioned across to Louie.

I watched in horror as Marcus tipped over the lip of the pit and disappeared into the seething mass of bodies.

"No!"

I stopped thinking about anything except Marcus in that moment. Rocco Durant, the other goons, the fact that I was in a slaughterhouse turned vampire production facility—it all disappeared. The only things that were real in my mind were Marcus and the pit. I had to get him out of there, no matter the consequences.

I had saved him once. I could save him again.

Jerking the sword away from Rocco, I leaned forward, springing with all my might toward shrieking oblivion. At the height of my jump, the pit looked to be a thousand feet deep.

I could see Marcus bound on the floor. They hadn't gotten to him yet.

I still had time.

## 26

I ROLLED ON THE LANDING, narrowly avoiding a savage kick to the face from someone in the full thrall of vampire madness. Down here, the noise was even worse. All the agonized voices weaved together into a tapestry of torment.

*Rocco Durant, you are so dead*, I vowed silently. After I found Marcus, freed him, and figured out a way to get the hell out of here alive.

In my head, it sounded like madness. Out loud, it would also have sounded like madness, but I refused to leave Marcus to die like this. I had already made my choice in a pretty irreversible way.

Good thing I still had the sword.

The blade took its first casualty as it flamed into existence, cleaving someone behind me in half. I only knew this because I felt the telltale sizzle of its cutting, and I heard the thump of the corpse falling among its brethren. The smell of fresh blood sparked a frenzy around me, but since I had none on me by virtue of the sword, the vampires-to-be didn't seem too interested in me.

I was thankful for that, though there was no time to dwell on it. I aimed myself in my best approximation of the direction Marcus was in and started swinging in wide, looping arcs that took as much advantage of momentum as possible. The masses began to drop like flies, and the wailing built to a fever pitch. I could feel it in my teeth. I thought my head was going to split apart or shatter.

I didn't look, but I had no doubt Rocco was watching. That made me all the more determined to succeed. Someone had to show him how deranged this all was. Someone had to make him pay.

I was happy to volunteer myself.

With the sword in front of me, I shouldered aggressively through the crowd. It was some kind of horrible, grisly mosh pit where instead of dancing like bulldozers, the participants ripped and devoured each other. They didn't seem to like the fiery nature of the sword, which worked to my advantage, but I discovered real fast that some of them didn't care.

A pair of terrifyingly strong hands gripped my shoulders. I yelped in pain as they twisted me around to face their owner, a gaunt, impossibly pale woman whose budding fangs had torn through her lower lip. She stared at me for a long second, her clouded eyes blank. Then she dove in for my neck.

I ran her through without questioning the action, without even feeling the heft of the sword in my arm. She died, her hot breath on my skin. So close. I had come so close to the most excruciating kind of death I had ever seen.

My hand shook so badly I nearly dropped the sword. I took a deep breath, held it tighter, and pressed on.

All I cared about was getting out of the hell Rocco Durant had created. And then I was resolved to send him to it.

---

As I THOUGHT I got closer to where Marcus might be, I started calling his name over the unbearable din so that if he was still alive, he'd know I was coming to get him.

"Marcus!"

Other than alerting my friend to my presence, the one word became a mantra for me to keep some of my sanity.

"Marcus!"

As long as I could call him and know who I was calling, I was still myself. That helped so much. It also helped that eventually, I heard a response.

"Vic!"

My heart leapt. "Marcus! I'm almost there!"

Two creatures wrestled violently in front of me, bashing into others and blocking my path. With a frustrated roar, I drew back and cut them all down together. They fell in a jumble of bony limbs, and I shoved my way around them.

A hand grabbed my ankle. I liberated it from its grasp. Some guy turned around and screeched in my face, so I put a hole through to the back of his skull.

Objectively, on some far-removed plane, I knew it was

all horrific, and these memories would have to be suppressed or else I'd run the risk of losing my mind when it was all over. But in the moment, I was so oversaturated with images of death and gore that it hardly seemed to register after the first few minutes. It was like I put myself in a box, armored by the necessity of my mission, and that box protected me from all else.

Sort of like the way I'd been steamrolling my way through life for half a decade.

I did a lot more slashing, more swearing, and more indiscriminate shoving. The sword whistled and hummed around me as it helped me do the worst work I'd ever done. I had commanded my brain not to think about the fact that these had been people at one point, not long in the past. Real people, with families, and homes, and pets.

All gone now. These creatures were no longer human. Because of Rocco Durant and that shitkicker Delano. He'd have to be dealt with, too, ultimately.

*Not yet. Don't think too far ahead. Find Marcus.*

I'd gotten far enough that Marcus was easily findable. He'd worked himself into a kneeling position, and whenever a hungry creature got too close, he'd clobber it with the heavy shackles on his wrists. I had to admire his ingenuity. He was bloody, but his wits had kept him alive so far.

When he saw me push through the last layer of the once-human blockade, his whole face lit up. He was looking older again, his hair fine and almost completely gray. The lines around his mouth and eyes had never looked so deep.

It scared me, but he brought me out of it by holding out his arms so that I could see the irons. "Cut them off, Vic, quickly! Then we fight our way out!" His tone was jarringly jovial.

I sliced through the manacles, and then I did the same for the cuffs on his ankles. He stood up immediately, shaking the blood back into his extremities. "Are you looking forward to this?" I shouted. "Because I'm not!"

"My thanks!" he answered back. "Fear not, Vic! In battle is the most noble way for men—and women—to die!"

That did not help. It *did* help to have my friend back, though. His naturally buoyant spirit lifted me up from the slag heap of human misery that was threatening to consume us both. I glanced at the sword in my hand. Should I have given it back? Marcus hadn't asked, and I was getting used to the feel of the thing. Plus, I had no other weapon.

There were much fewer vampire prototypes in the pit now, thanks to my rampaging quest to find Marcus, but the remaining creatures still looked like a lot, and with less of the others to occupy them, they focused their intensity on us.

"Stay close to me!" Marcus called over his shoulder. "If we separate, we cannot help each other!"

I backed up until my shoulders were almost touching his, and I brandished the sword. The horde surged toward us, drooling and glaring with their clawed hands outstretched. Their teeth gleamed with a ghastly, hellish glow when they got in range of my sword's light. I sucked in a deep breath, let it out, and willed my mind to stabilize.

My eyes closed for a moment, and when I opened them, I felt like a renewed person.

"Let's do this."

The sword burned through the air, drawing designs with the afterglow of its strikes. The embers from burning remains danced around us, smoldering when they hit the ground, erupting into flames when they came in contact with hair, clothes, or, occasionally, papery skin. I became slowly but surely inured to the constant droning screams of the damned, to the point where I either didn't hear it anymore or I'd gone deaf.

It wouldn't have made a difference either way. My only purpose in life had become to escape the pit. I could think about everything else when it became relevant again.

On my right, Marcus moved like a well-oiled machine, demonstrating the techniques he had been trying to teach me in flawless fashion. Although he was fighting without the blessed weapon of a god, he cut down his shrieking foes in equal, if not greater numbers. The corpses were starting to pile up around us, like horrid snowdrifts. Many of them were beginning to crumble away, but not all. It was helpful, in a way. It kept the living from approaching in any direction other than straight on.

They fell without much effort on my part. Kronin's blade made short work of them. I had never seen so many shining examples of a humanoid body reduced to its parts, nor had I imagined myself becoming so accustomed to it. The tricky part was when they decided to swarm, which seemed to be happening with greater and greater regularity. Then, I had to pull out the fancy maneuvers, less reliable than my good old slash-and-hack method.

I whipped the sword over my head, bringing it down in a crazy spin. Biological shrapnel scattered in every direction, pelting the next wave of proto-vamps as they began their assault. It was grim as hell, but it got results. I felt myself deadening inside.

"Good, Vic!" Marcus bellowed over the din of his own attacks. "You are much improving!"

I glanced toward him just in time to see him fell three of the vamplets in quick succession. The guy was in beast mode.

I *had* been in beast mode, but my stamina was beginning to falter. All my sword slinging muscles burned. I couldn't believe the thing was so damn heavy. Exhaustion threatened to overcome the limited reserves of adrenaline still struggling to supply my body with the energy I needed to keep going. The sword seemed to gain a pound with every swing.

How much longer could I keep it up?

During a rare reprieve, I leaned the blade on the floor of the pit and bent over to catch my breath. That was when I noticed the blood all over my hands and arms, running down my legs, and seeping out through ragged holes in my clothing. I had no recollection of ever being hit, but it was unrealistic to expect to emerge from this encounter unscathed.

"Marcus." I felt wobbly on my feet. "I don't think I'm doing so good." The lull in action had given my body time to process and expel the rest of the adrenaline. I was shaky and spent.

More were still coming. *Damn it to hell.* How many were there?

"Rally, Vic!" He came over and helped me straighten up. "Draw power from your wounds. When the battle is through, there will be plenty of time to rest and recover, but we have not yet broken onto the other side." He looked up. "Not much longer. I will handle the bulk of the rest."

I nodded. "Thank you." My vision blurred as I labored to steady myself under the sword. I saw the fiery blade weaving back and forth. In the field of the emptying pit before me, a single vampire came into focus. She was bigger than most of the others had been, her arms and hands more developed. The points of her nails dripped with someone else's blood.

She had battle scars.

"I don't think you're part of this class," I said, mostly to myself. She wasn't listening, even if she could hear my weak, raspy voice. Her eyes were not as cloudy and dazed as the others. She was focused right on my face.

I barely managed to track her after she jumped. My downward chop with the sword was ninety percent estimated. It found some part of her, but not before those nails had gouged their way down through the already-injured flesh of my upper chest. I looked down in shock and saw her hand, driven down to the knuckle, sticking out of my skin. The fingers twitched.

I screamed.

Much of what happened after that was a blur. I started to bleed in a serious way, and Marcus, alerted by my screaming, went into berserker overdrive. He was the one who finished off the last of the stragglers, assessed my injury, and half-hauled my ass out of there. The pit was closing as we neared the top. I remembered the rumble of the cover inching its way toward us. Marcus cut an opening in the edge with the sword.

He laid me out on the slaughterhouse floor, face up,

with the hideous gashes in my flesh exposed for the world to see. The chamber was eerily quiet. The soundproof doors must have been closed, and Rocco was nowhere to be found. He'd probably split after I jumped into the pit, thinking his job was done.

We were alone.

"Relax your breathing," Marcus told me. "Heavy aspiration may trigger your heart to enter a state of panic, which will only increase your blood loss." He smiled. His face was blurred over my head. "I have seen worse in my time. Everything will be all right."

I wasn't sure I believed him, but it was nice to hear, even if I knew that my life was flowing out of me at a steady pace. I let my eyes fall closed until I felt him leaning over me again. "Drink this," he said and tilted his open flask into my mouth.

The liquid inside was thick and sweet, like honey mixed with flowers. At first, I could barely get it down, but then, it began to fill me with a warmth that blotted out the pain. My eyelids grew so heavy I could no longer open them, but this fact did not bother me at all. I was perfectly content to lay there as my body did… something.

Marcus's voice floated into my consciousness on a cloud. "Be still, Vic. You are healing. You must let your body mend for a time."

*That's fine*, I wanted to say. My lips wouldn't form the words. The warmth pulled me gently down toward deep, enveloping sleep.

Then a different force kicked in. I was immediately elevated out of dreamland, wide awake and riding a tsunami of the most incredible power I'd ever felt. I tried to call out to Marcus and ask him what was happening, but I still couldn't speak, move, or open my eyes. It was less soothing now.

The tsunami swelled over me, crashing around and through my body. Its wild strength infused into my bones, my muscles, and my spirit.

I could feel it changing me.

I could also feel Marcus moving around. His footsteps presented visually in my mind. I traced his progress, circling me, checking the door, and looking down into the pit in case we had missed any of Rocco's fleet of vampires. Marcus looked alarmingly weak to me, but I chalked it up to my own exhaustion. He just needed time to get back to full force. Even soldiers chosen by the gods had their limits.

I didn't know it at the time, but I became aware of Rocco's renewed presence long before Marcus did. The mob boss approached from the other side of the double doors, and I tried my best to warn Marcus somehow, but I couldn't make my body do anything, despite the electric current of energy Marcus's flask had given me.

Marcus was standing with his back to the doors when Rocco hit him.

Trapped in my healing body, I screamed without a voice. I struggled to force my limbs to respond to my commands. Nothing worked. My eyes were still closed, but I could see them in my mind.

Marcus was losing.

## 27

IF I HAD KNOWN Marcus was so weak, I never would have let him fight. I would have dragged myself up out of that pit or died trying. I wouldn't have allowed him to shoulder the burden of saving me. I didn't know he was just going to get his ass beat by Rocco Durant.

By the time I realized what was happening, it was too late. Marcus was matched in stature to Rocco, but not in weight, and his strength was starting to flicker out. He had not had the sword hilt in his hand when Rocco attacked, and the first thing Rocco did was wrench it off Marcus's belt and toss it out of reach of both of them.

"You and me," he said, smiling that awful smile. "Fair fight. Let's go."

It wasn't a fair fight. I knew it as I lay some feet away, swimming through a daze of healing. In my trance state, I had the ability to understand how strong they were on a level that was deeper than squats and bench presses. It was a weird glimpse into a world I had never even considered before.

I could see the vitality of Marcus's spirit, and I also knew that spirit was slipping away.

Not because of Rocco, but because of the wound in his back. It had spread while we were separated, and now, I caught sight of it whenever Marcus's back was to me, a network of dark veins spiderwebbing hungrily over his torso. The wound he had suffered in Carcerum was consuming him.

I didn't want to watch Marcus die, but my eyes stayed glued to the fight, even as the tears well up under my eyelids. Rocco's punches were hard and unforgiving, frighteningly relentless. Marcus's weakening form gave way under his might. It wasn't even. Rocco Durant had become a vampire and harnessed the full strength burgeoning in the ones we had slaughtered in the pit. He would not stop unless pierced through the heart or taken apart by the sword.

I knew this as surely as I knew my own name. And that knowledge followed me as I broke through the surface, back into the waking world.

---

MY BODY still wouldn't work, but I was fully present in it again, and I could open my eyes. The space just above my heart that the vamp lady had tried to vent for me no longer felt like it was releasing my soul into the next realm. I knew I was very close to moving. Just not quite there.

Marcus lay limp under Rocco's pummeling strikes as

the mob boss finally began to slow down. He was panting, gasping, and coughing. I wished a heart attack on him right then and there, but it failed to materialize, like so many of my other wishes.

Instead, the large man crawled, wheezing, off of Marcus and shambled over to me.

"Good," he said, upon looking down into my face. "You're awake. I'd hate for you to miss this." His hand ran a sleazy path over my leg that made me flush with rage and disgust. His gaze traveled down my body. "I meant what I said, you know?" He lowered his voice. "You're not a bad looker, kid. What do you say we make the most of our time together, huh?"

If I could have thrown up, I would have. I'd never asked for an extreme close up of Rocco Durant's face, but I was getting an extended one as he leered over me. I knew exactly what he was thinking; I could see it in his ugly, lecherous mug. I would rather die than let him do that to me.

I had a plan brewing, though, and sometimes, plans require a little sacrifice. Or a lot.

"You're gorgeous when you can't talk, sweetheart. I bet you've heard that one before." He chuckled at himself and smoothed the tattered remains of my shirt. "Looks like my little pets did most of the job for me, huh? Before you killed them all, that is." His grin widened into a shark's rictus. "I'm impressed, little lady. Most people woulda been chum inside of ten seconds if they ever did something as stupid as you did. I'm not sure you know how lucky you are. That's all right. Rocco will teach ya."

It took him a minute to heave his bulk across me, but

then, Rocco Durant was straddling my hips and pressing his weight down on me. I felt my diaphragm straining to inflate. My heart beat faster.

*Get off me, dickhole.*

"Oh, I'm sorry." The smile never left his face. "Are you having trouble breathing? Get used to it, girlie, because that's how I like 'em. Makes it harder for you to fight back." He patted his belly. "I'm a little past my fighting days, see. Now I prefer submission."

*Ugh.* I commanded my hand to ball into a fist. To my profound relief and delight, it did. *Yes!* I was that much closer to getting myself out of this.

Rocco reached down and grabbed my arms, one of each in his monster mitts. "Lemme help ya, sweetie. Life ain't nothin' without a little romance, am I right?" He wrapped my arms around his generous waist, and he propped himself up over me. The gaudy tie hit me in the face.

He laughed.

I let him amuse himself with that, despite the fact that I would have liked nothing more than to throttle him with it. He didn't notice my hands creeping ever so slowly down to his back pocket, which had been made baggy, presumably by a bankroll or wallet the size of a paperback novel. The outline of something precious stood out against the fabric. Two more of those syringes.

*Should have kept them all in your jacket, Casanova.*

I withdrew my hand with the patience of a surgeon, enduring a thorough and much too close examination of my facial features. His thumb mapped my cheeks and jaw.

"I think you're gonna make one hell of a specimen, toots," he said. "I sure hope you live through it. You might be the one who helps us fulfill god's master plan in the end." He sat up. I gasped a little as more air was squeezed out of me. "Imagine it. You saw the fury of those pesky little shitbags up close, and that was only Stage One. We're gonna have an army of full-fledged vamps. Hundreds of thousands of 'em laying waste to the human world." He shook his head in greasy wonder. "I never realized how completely useless humans were. Don't do nothing except eat, piss, shit, and screw. Work? Means nothing. Money? Means nothing. You're still gonna die someday.

"Vamps don't have that problem. And now, I'm one of 'em, so neither do I. And soon, that'll be you, too." He patted my cheek a little harder than strictly necessary. "Look alive, sweet cheeks! It's the best damn day of your life."

It sure was, but not for the reasons he thought.

With an effort that would have been lauded by Kronin himself, I heaved my waking arm up from where I'd let it fall off his back. The syringe from his pocket sat soldier-ready in my hand. Coordination was still something of a problem, but he had a neck like a damn Sequoia, and that made things easier for me. I felt the needle hit home. Not exactly where I wanted it, but close enough.

Rocco's eyes nearly popped out of his head. I held the plunger down for as long as I could, and then I dropped it. He fumbled at the needle in his neck. "You... you..."

His hands slapped the floor, pushing him away from me. I watched him stagger backward, half crouched, his thick arms outstretched.

My tongue formed two crucial syllables in my mouth. The only two I needed.

"*Fuck you.*"

He didn't respond outside of more incoherent babbling. A thread of drool hung from the corner of his mouth. "What… what have you done?"

I eased myself up on my hands. The motion was flooding back into my body. I felt better than ever.

"From the looks of it," I said. "I just killed you."

Then, Rocco Durant did something I did not like at all.

He started to laugh.

It began as a high-pitched, wheezy giggle that deepened gradually into something more coarse and malicious, a regular devil laugh. That was around the point where I wondered if I might have made a mistake. I had assumed that another whole vial of concentrated vampire blood would just destroy him outright.

It was looking like that was not the case.

"Shit." I got to my feet in a hurry, backing away from him. All his blood vessels popped out under his skin, a network of red and blue. The skin itself had flushed almost purple over the course of about thirty seconds. Even the capillaries in his eyes bulged.

"Shit!" I said again. I turned and ran for the sword.

I knew where it was; it had skidded into a corner after Rocco threw it. So, the issue wasn't its location as much as it was my speed. I thought I was moving faster than I'd ever moved in my life, even at a half strength, I-just-woke-up-from-a-healing-coma lope, but unless my ears deceived me, Rocco Durant was on the chase.

He was a fast old bastard now, thanks to my quick thinking. How was I supposed to know the benefits of vampire blood were stacking, not fatal?

I never ceased to amaze myself with my own innate ability to screw things up.

Somehow, I got to the sword, and I picked it up. It was burning by the time I turned back to face Rocco. I didn't want to start off this fight trapped in a corner. Maybe he'd be twice as tall now. Or have four legs or four arms. Claws, a tail, horns that shot venom? It was all fair game as far as I knew.

Not even this open-minded approach was enough to prepare me for Rocco Durant's second vamp transformation. I felt my mouth drop open as I took him in.

Nope. No. Absolutely not.

This was not what I had signed up for.

## 28

THE MONSTROSITY formerly known as Rocco Durant towered over me, its hulking shoulders dwarfed by a pair of leathery wings that stretched out six feet in either direction. His face was a grotesque amalgamation of the one I knew mixed with a wild animal's. Sickly pale, almost translucent skin stretched over a brand-new jaw from which a crop of fangs bristled unevenly.

I was pretty sure he wasn't supposed to look like that. Clearly, I'd messed with vamp evolution by overloading him.

Every bit of exposed skin gleamed with a disgusting, slimy sheen. The long, grotesque fingers ended in ragged nails that were slightly curved on the ends, and obviously razor sharp. I thought back to the vamp in my loft, trying to get at me with a similar configuration. Hopefully, these would prove equally unwieldy.

I started to move in, keeping my eyes on as many points of danger as I could. The sword didn't feel so heavy anymore—almost the same as the training sword I used with Marcus.

*Marcus.*

My eyes flicked to his body, lying where he had been taken down. His eyes were closed. He looked ragged, like a fresh corpse. But to my surprise, his chest hitched as it rose and fell. The tough old grandpa was still hanging on.

*Okay, Vic,* I told myself. *You know what to do. Make this fast.*

Marcus's life still hung in the balance. I still had a chance to save him.

Rocco watched me with freakish eyes that seemed like they were popping out of his face. The sockets stretched nightmarishly to contain them. They resembled bat eyes. I wondered if he was blind or half blind.

At this point, I'd take either.

His lower half was heavy and strangely proportioned. Giant feet on muscular legs tapered up to a confusingly tiny waist. If I could mess with his center of balance and get him to roll on his back, killing him would be a piece of vampire cake. I'd have to get him on the ground anyway. His body had contorted and grown to nearly ten feet, too tall to try the upward thrust that had worked so well before.

Why did Rocco Durant have to make everything so complicated, right up until the bitter end?

"Hey!" I shouted. I even waved the sword to help him locate me, in case those eyes really didn't do much for him. "Never thought I'd say this, but I liked you better before!" I gestured to my face. "That blood really messed you up in here, huh?"

The eyes narrowed into dark slits. I smirked. He was too vain to suffer insults about his appearance lightly, even in gross monster form, which was weird because he had always been staggeringly ugly.

I expected him to come shambling forward, but he moved with a surprisingly lithe kind of grace, like a predator built for one purpose. Whenever he moved, light glinted off the fangs fighting to burst from behind his pallid lips. There were way more than two crammed in that horrible maw. Could I afford to get close enough to stab him without getting bit?

It was a chance I really didn't want to take, but I didn't have much of a choice. The stabby plan was the only plan. *Let's just hope he cooperates long enough to die.*

We circled each other warily. His huge black eyes were glued to my face. In their bottomless depths, I thought I caught the sense of something moving. A shudder passed down my spine. He wasn't as big as I might have expected, but damn, he was creepy. And something told me he was going to be dangerously fast.

Soon enough, he proved my hunch correct. I only had a split second to catch him gearing up for the charge, but it was just barely enough. He came flashing toward me in a hideous blur, and I got ready to try and nail the right timing.

I'd always been athletic, my training had only increased my natural abilities, so I felt like I had a decent chance of at least moderate success. But man, he was quick. I felt him pass just under the flat of my blade. *Damn it to hell!*

My one saving grace was that I somehow followed through at a rate of speed at least approaching Rocco's. I tracked his progress with supernatural ease through eyes that had been seeing double and triple only twenty minutes before. As he looped around for the second pass, I planted my feet like rocks, steeling myself for the strike. No wonder Marcus chugged that stuff in his flask all the time. It made me feel like a superhero.

Rocco's eyes were set in obsidian slits. His posture began to change as he approached me, and I put it together that he was getting ready to pounce. Maybe he thought the sudden movement would throw me off enough that I'd screw up and impale myself or something. I had to admire his level of optimism. Little did he know how well the sword responded to me post-healing. It felt almost like an extension of my own body.

The second time he blew past me, I sliced at him with greater precision, a honed sense of purpose. The tip of the sword struck something; I felt the tiniest bit of resistance at the top of the swing. Rocco made a high hissing sound, which I soon realized was the noise made by a stream of ash falling from a gash in his upper arm. He clutched at it with one freakish hand, glowering at me.

I made a show of shaking off the sword. He didn't like that, which meant I loved it. But knowing how fast he had presented me with my main problem—how to pin him down long enough to put the blade in his heart. He did not need to be told that slowing down was as good as death, if skill and luck were on my side.

I found myself perversely enjoying the puzzle of strength and logic. Was I actually having fun while Marcus clung to life on the floor? *He'd be having more fun than me.*

Until I got the old soldier back in working order, I'd

have to have enough fun for the both of us. Clasping the god-king's weapon in my right hand, I advanced on Rocco's position. He still held onto his injured arm, staring at me with those unsettling jet-black eyes. There was no telling how much he saw, or what the world looked like to him.

Obviously, he could kill me if I made a wrong move. Also, obviously, he looked a little different than he used to. But he had always been able to kill me if I made a mistake, and so far, I'd scraped by. There was no need to be more afraid of him now that he was like Nosferatu's crackhead cousin.

But he was still alive, and I needed to solve that problem before he figured out a way to solve his. He seemed to be most comfortable strafing me, relying on his crazy speed to keep him out of harm's way. If I could stop him from moving somehow, I had a feeling I'd obtain the upper hand. And what better way to stop him than by using brute force?

It was my favorite strategy.

I kept creeping toward Rocco, pretending like I didn't know exactly what he wanted to do. His hand fell away from the wound on his arm as he prepared to sprint at me again. Every time my blade twitched, it drew his inky gaze. I made a note of that—a distraction that could be used to my advantage. At the moment, however, I wanted to lull him into a false sense of security.

So, I stopped. Unsure of what my game was, he stopped too.

We stared each other down in a few perfect moments of stillness.

Then he came rocketing for me, claws and teeth flashing. I sent the sword on a wild goose chase through the air as I dodged, missing his gaunt form handily. He grinned, and that was when I recognized him most. Still made my skin crawl.

We effectively swapped positions.

"Is that all you got, you vamped-up piece of shit?" I taunted him as I scrambled backward.

A smile spread on his face. He broke into a hideous laugh. "I don't need much more. You are just a spoiled little bitch. Me? I've transcended humanity."

Rocco raised his thick arms as he cut a wide circle around me. He clearly thought he was homing in for the kill, but he was mistaken. Finally, the tables were turning in the culmination of our five-year fight.

He didn't know it yet, but Rocco no longer had the upper hand.

"Come on then!" I screamed. My eyes narrowed in rage. "Let's end this."

I traced his trajectory with my new, steady eyes, pinpointing his exact location a few seconds into the future. Then it was my turn to run, blazing forward on stronger, faster legs. Rocco wasn't the only one who was fast as hell. And by the time he learned, it was way too late.

The force of the collision sent us both flying into the wall. The building shuddered on impact. Wheezing, Rocco slashed furiously with his deadly nails, trying to get to my throat. I shoved back from him, answering his flailing with stabs of my own. Even confined between me and the wall, he was still fast. The point of the sword cascaded sparks whenever it struck the wall instead of Rocco.

A wayward nail caught me just barely in the face, opening a long scratch over my cheek. I winced enough for Rocco to push me backward. We tumbled to the ground, still tearing at each other. Not the way I had envisioned things to go, but I was nothing if not a scrapper. Still, he was strong, and I struggled to get over top of him. The hideous caricature of his face, hairless and leering, loomed over mine. A thread of saliva hung from the corner of his mouth.

"It's over. You're the kill I will never forget." He spoke with hot foul breath.

He pinned the hilt of Kronin's sword up against my body, the blade so close to my face that I could hear it humming and feel the edge of its searing heat. Beads of sweat stood out on my skin. If it even touched me, I was sure I'd die. The thing was made to kill monsters; I'd seen what it did to humans. Every muscle in my body strained to keep it away from me.

Every muscle in Rocco's body strained for the opposite. There was only one way this temporary stalemate could end.

I looked deep into his black, emotionless eyes, searching for any remnant of the man he used to be. All I needed was a shred of the hate I felt for him to ignite a wildfire within my soul. If I could get to that place, I could win. Because deep down, it wasn't about Rocco Durant the vampire. He hadn't been a vampire when he shot my parents.

He had just been a good-for-nothing sack of shit. And that was who I needed to kill.

"I know you're in there," I told him around clenched teeth. "And the second I see you—you're as good as dead!"

At first, there was nothing. Just pupil-less black orbs. Then, something vague stirred down inside them. Something I recognized from that night at the docks when I had my gun up in his face.

The ghost of fear.

His merciless grip loosened almost imperceptibly, but I felt it. I lunged with all the strength in my body, sending him splaying supine across the floor. My momentum, unchecked, carried me up and over, into the position for which I had been battling unsuccessfully. Now I was the one looking down in triumph, Rocco's mutilated face cast in the fiery glow of the god-king's sword.

His black eyes bugged out. We both knew it was the end of the line.

"No. It is I that will remember." Strength of the gods surged through me. I knew it was over. "Now go rot in hell, where you belong."

Kronin's sword went straight into his heart. The death was so instantaneous that he only had time to open and close his mouth once. Like before, his features sort of slipped back toward normal as he died, then disintegrated.

I felt no remorse at all.

---

THE PILE of ash from Rocco Durant spread over the bare concrete, as if even his base atoms couldn't bear to be near each other any longer. I leapt to my feet and ran until I could drop to my knees at Marcus' side.

"Hey," I said urgently, resisting the desperate urge to shake him. "Marcus. Can you hear me? It's Vic."

He looked worse than before. My heart told me he was halfway through death's door, but I couldn't bring myself to give up on him.

"Vic." He spoke just above a whisper and tried to smile.

"Wait. Quiet. I got you." I looked around for his flask, spotted it, and snatched it up. "Here. This will fix you, right? It fixed the *hell* out of me."

I frowned. Something didn't feel right. I shook the vessel a little.

It was empty.

"Oh, Marcus," I whispered. "No."

## 29

"WHY?" I bent over him and took his hand. It was cold in mine. "You gave me the last of it. *Why?*"

The tears in my eyes made his face swim. I wiped them away fiercely. I wanted to remember that face for the rest of my damned life.

Marcus took a labored breath. "Forgive me, Vic. I did not tell you..." He trailed off, took another breath, and resumed. "The wound I sustained in Carcerum was *always* going to kill me. There is no escaping Lorcan's curse."

"Lorcan?" I frowned. "You said he wasn't the god of death. You said he couldn't do that."

"Anyone can kill," Marcus answered. "You know that now."

I blinked back the tears. "This can't be happening. There wasn't enough time. And I acted like such an ass."

"Perhaps that is a fault which lies with us both." He gripped my hand harder. "Now, listen. I do not have much longer."

I sat back. "Okay." Just this once, I could do what he asked and listen. I owed it to him.

"Do not be angry with me," he began. "It is too late for that. But someone had to drink the nectar. And I chose you." He indicated the flask with his other hand. "That has imbued the strength of Carcerum unto you. You must take up my mantle and fulfill my mission." A sigh escaped him, and I leaned down again, petrified that I was on the verge of losing him. "I am sorry. It was a dishonorable way to do it, but I had no choice. I wanted to save you."

A tear escaped and rolled down my cheek. "*Me?*"

"You." His smile turned sad. "Do not weep for me. Weep for the people I was unable to save. And then avenge them. Protect your people."

"But..." I grappled with the reality of what was happening. There had to be some way to stop it, to trigger the magic that would let Marcus stay. "But we never found your warrior. What about the yogurt guy?"

He laughed fitfully. "You're still so dense. I *did* find my warrior." His eyes softened. "She's looking right at me. It was *always* you. But I was too blind..."

As his words dawned on me, a strange burden settled on my mind.

"I'm not ready." I didn't know why I kept protesting except that I wanted Marcus to remain a little longer. "Also, you said the warrior had to spar with you. We never did that."

"Yes, we did. In practice, perhaps, but your spirit was so fierce that it mattered not." He squeezed my hand again. "Tell me you will accept it, Vic. Tell me you will strive to love this world in the way it deserves. Find the gods, banish them. Let your noble people live in peace."

More tears had started to fall. "We're not noble," I said, my voice cracking. "But you are. And your nobility, it gives me hope. If you want me to take up the mantle, I will."

"Thank you." He blinked, but his eyes stayed closed for such a long time that I started to panic.

"Marcus? Marcus."

"Did you know?" He opened his eyes halfway. "In Rome, we Centurions were given more than one name. Two, sometimes three. Do you have a name other than Vic?"

Confused, I answered without thinking. "Victoria."

He smiled. "My second name… was Victorius."

I lost it. I couldn't help it. I tried to stem the sobs for fear that he would die while I was bawling over him, but they just wouldn't be contained. Even though it hurt like crazy, it was also cleansing.

"I can't believe you're leaving me," I sobbed. "Don't."

He moved his hand a little. "I'll never leave you, Victoria. Remember what I said. And… protect the people."

"How? I don't know anything."

Marcus squeezed my hand, and he said it again. "Protect the people."

Then his eyes closed. His hand went limp in mine.

And he was gone.

---

What happened directly after Marcus died happened so quickly that I wasn't sure I was seeing it or just imagining. I saw it in his face first.

I was horrified, but the shock morphed quickly into wonder.

The aging process I had seen before began anew, but rapidly. His eyes sank into his skull, his skin loosened, and his lips disappeared. The hand still holding mine grew frail and brittle. His true age came through in a body that had carried him for thousands of years.

I didn't let go until it was little more than bones wrapped in skin.

Marcus Victorius, First Cohort of the Roman Army, faded from Earth somewhat less obtrusively than he had arrived on it after an interval of two thousand years. He left me kneeling on the second floor of a newly re-abandoned slaughterhouse, head down, weeping softly into my lap.

I felt so very alone.

I didn't know how long I stayed there, folded up beside the place where my friend had spent his last minutes. The next leg of the journey had to begin without him, and I didn't want to do it. I wanted to find somewhere soft and warm and dark, crawl in, curl up, and sleep until nothing hurt and I was whole again.

I couldn't do that, so instead, I stood up to go home. The waning afternoon light caught on a piece of metal on the floor.

I gasped.

It was Marcus's medallion.

Cautiously, I leaned down and picked it up, cradling it in my hands. The coat of arms gleamed up at me. I traced its curved lines with my fingers, and I remembered what Marcus had said about it.

*It is said to keep the spirits of my father and our ancestors close, should I need them.*

Well, Marcus was not my dad, but he *had* left this treasure for me, and I was determined to honor him through it. I lifted the golden chain and put it around my neck. The medallion settled beside my heart. It was warm, and then it got warmer. A glow that matched his hero-king's sword emanated from the golden engraving.

Comforting.

A breeze passed through the room, spiraling in through one of many broken windows. I heard a familiar voice tug at the back of my mind.

I jumped in shock, and then began laughing. It was a sweet, joyous sound, and it echoed through the room.

Shaking my head, I said, "You and your damn magic keeps surprising me."

*Ah, Vic*, Marcus said in my mind. *At long last, you believe.*

I smiled. "Yeah. I guess I do."

*Good. Then let's go kill some gods.*

# EPILOGUE

THE DEMIGOD STOOD with his back straight, his hands clasped behind him and looking out the picture window of the office on the top floor. His master was behind the desk like always, turned away from him. Lorcan did not like to talk to others' faces unless the matter was very grave. He preferred the aura of mystery inherent to his myth, particularly now that he was free to roam at will, no longer confined to Carcerum.

What sweet freedom it was.

"My Lord," Delano said softly, deferentially. "I have news."

"Good?" Lorcan asked.

Delano sighed. "And bad, my Lord. I am sorry we have disappointed you."

"Indeed." Lorcan drummed his gloved fingers on the arm of his chair. "Begin with the positive."

"The Centurion has been found—and killed."

Lorcan smiled wide, his fingers coming to a rest. "This

is excellent news indeed. That fool Marcus, always Kronin's favorite pet. It's a pity I didn't get to witness his demise myself. But no matter. How did you fail me?"

"We have lost one of our locations." Delano braced himself for a burst of Lorcan's infamous temper, which, though rare, was the stuff of legends.

Before Carcerum, Lorcan had engulfed an entire citadel in the realm of shadow in order to punish a wayward king. He had extinguished towns by depriving them of light, just as a token of his displeasure.

Delano admired him so very much.

"Which one?" Lorcan's fingers began to drum again. His voice betrayed no hint of emotion. "Not the slaughter-house, I hope."

Delano winced. "It... was the slaughterhouse, my Lord."

He half suspected that Lorcan already knew and simply asked just to make his servant uncomfortable. It was part of his nature, after all. Not even his friends were exempt from the barest hints of his malice. Lorcan considered it a gift. To himself, as well as to others.

Now, the greater god sighed with melodramatic flair. "Oh, and there was so much potential there." He turned his chair a few degrees. "Why is it, my dear Delano, that forces consistently oppose my plans?" The chair inched around a little more. "Which one of the greater beings accomplished this? Don't fear. I know it wasn't you. You are my most faithful, purest sycophant."

"I am, my Lord." Delano grimaced. "But it wasn't at the hand of a god or an Apprenti. A human destroyed the plant."

"A human?" Lorcan fought the urge to rub his temples. "How did he accomplish this?"

"*She*, actually my Lord. I believe that the woman was working with the Roman."

Lorcan nodded, a sick feeling suddenly coming over him. He felt he knew the answer to his next question before he asked it.

"What are you not telling me, Delano? Even with Marcus's help, she should not have been able to stop that rat Durant, not after he had my blood pumped into his veins."

"You're right, my lord. As always." Delano played his part perfectly. He had not clawed his way this far up the ranks through dumb luck alone. He knew exactly how to fill Lorcan's intentional silences, how to massage the ego of a god, and how to turn his phrases so that Lorcan would listen without ripping his head off. He was very good at his job. "The woman, she possesses the *Gladius Solis*."

The name of Kronin's sword cast a pall over the room. Lorcan swiveled back toward the window, sulking. Since the fall of Carcerum, he had allowed himself the hope that the cursed instrument had been destroyed. To know that it had fallen into the hands of a human woman was simply unacceptable.

The chair turned ever so slightly. The shadow of Lorcan's legs was visible now, long and trim in precisely pressed black trousers. For a being who so seldom deigned to be in the view of others, he took great pride in his appearance.

"Delano."

"My Lord?"

"Tell me you know what your next mission will be."

Delano smiled slightly. "I can guess, my Lord. None of our weapons will matter as long as she, or one of the other gods, is in possession of the sword."

"Correct," said Lorcan. "So?"

"So, I will bring the sword to you, my Lord."

"Amazing." Lorcan settled back into his chair with a smile, the tension leaving him. Delano always knew exactly what to say. "You never disappoint me, Delano."

"I strive not to, my Lord. And what shall I do with the girl? Releasing her would be most unwise." He couldn't imagine allowing a pest with her potential to go free, which was apparently exactly what Rocco Durant had done, the mutant dunce.

"You are correct once again, my servant. Bring the girl to me, along with the blade. I have a feeling that we will have much to discuss."

Delano inclined his head in total respect. "For you, Lord Lorcan, I will do anything."

"Yes." Lorcan's head returned to the proper position on his neck. His smile relaxed. He clapped his hands. "You, Delano, can do anything. And that is why you belong to me." He settled his hands in his lap, and the great chair rotated slowly back to face the view of the city below. "Such a wonderful, terrible, awful place, isn't it?" he observed absently.

"It is, my Lord."

Lorcan nodded. "I will be pleased when it has been burnt to the ground."

Dear Readers,

Thank you, thank you, thank you!

You've made it this far, and we are so glad you gave Forgotten Gods a shot!

Now, a little something about us. ST Branton, the author who wrote the book, is really the love child of dynamic duo Chris Raymond and Lee Barbant. Over the past several years, we've been writing together in the wee hours of the night and teaching together at the University during the day.

Frankly, I'm not sure how we haven't broken up yet!

So, after writing superhero books in the city of Pittsburgh (The Steel City Heroes), scifi thrillers across these United States (The Jack Carson Stories), and an epic eight book—and counting—magical fantasy taking place in the far future (The Rise of Magic), why the hell would we use a pen name?

Good question.

Well, there's plenty of reasons for it... but for now, let's just say, it is a rebranding for a fresh series.

Now, onto the official author notes.

I love writing. Love it. Really.

I love the fact that people want to read our stories, and Lee and I get to weave together tales about good and evil, with characters fraught with issues to overcome and dragons to slay (or gods to defeat). In the process they make both themselves and the world a better place.

I had dabbled in writing for years. Short stories. Crappy romantic poetry. Non-fiction. Academic mumbo-jumbo.

But my first real fiction books were written for my daughter Simone. She was young, but ahead of her years as a reader. Mrs. Raymond and I were at our wits end trying to find books she would enjoy with content we would approve. So, I figured, why not write some stories for my little girl! Months later, the Arcanum Island Series was born. (It has since been pulled for reworking and will be republished in Summer of 2018).

A year later, after a few drinks, Lee and I decided to write together. We made a pretty good run at it, sold a bunch of books, and had a load of fun in the process. But before long, we'd developed a friendship from afar with bestselling author Michael Anderle (The Kurtherian Gambit Universe) and somehow managed to talk him into letting us write in his world, which was teaming with possibilities (and readers!).

Michael's taught us a ton, most importantly about how to write a story that is kickass, while giving the readers what they're looking for when they grab a book. Hopefully, we're getting closer and closer.

Urban Fantasy has been one of my favorite genres for a long time. But before I met Harry Dresden or any other of the heavy hitting UF heroes, there were the gods. I grew up with a fascination with the Greek, Roman, and Egyptian pantheons. Pair that with a ridiculous amount of Dungeons and Dragons through my formative (non-dating years), and Vic and the Forgotten Gods series makes perfect sense!

There's a lot more coming. The layers of the Forgotten world will be peeled back in each book. I think you'll like what Vic will be facing in the next one!

Cheers!
Chris


PS: Since this is the first book in a new series, I'll make the shameless plug right off the bat. If you liked Forgotten Gods, please, please, please take a minute to drop a review on Amazon and pass along the recommendation to a friend. Thanks so much!

## AUTHOR NOTES - LEE BARBANT

### WRITTEN MARCH 7, 2018

Wow, what a great book, right? Such action. Such humor. Such heart. Of course, I'm more than a little biased. I helped write it after all.

For those of you who don't know me, my name is Lee Barbant (@lebarbant). I'm a new dad, a cat lover (specifically, a crotchety old tabby who hates the fact that I'm a new dad), and one part of the creative team behind ST Branton.

You've heard this from my partner already, but I wanted to start by first saying thank you so much for reading the book (and for reading these notes). We're really excited about this project, and the fact that you all gave it a chance means everything.

Secondly, I'd like to thank everyone on the <u>Forgotten Gods Facebook Group</u> who helped craft this story. Your input made this book what it is (for good or for bad. I personally blame you all if it fails).

If you're interested in supporting this project further,

please PLEASE, head on over to Amazon and leave the book a friendly review. Then check us out on Facebook. We're always looking for suggestions on how to improve our storytelling, and the folks in the group can tell you we take fan advice seriously.

OK, on to the next book.

For Kronin!
Lee

## CONNECT WITH THE AUTHORS

**Email List:**
http://www.subscribepage.com/smokeandsteelnews

**Facebook:**
Come hang out on the Forgotten Gods Facebook page:
https://www.facebook.com/ForgottenGodsSeries/

**Website:**
http://www.smokeandsteel.com

www.ingramcontent.com/pod-product-compliance
Lightning Source LLC
Chambersburg PA
CBHW050229110726
47898CB00007B/2082